I0671342

FRAMED

T.L. Joy &
Simone Majors

i

Framed

ISBN-13: 978-0692244555
Book cover Designed by: Kellie Dennis from Book Cover By Design
Published by Mahogany Publications
www.mahoganypublications.com

DEDICATION

This book is dedicated to all of our families, our friends, and our supporters. Thank you for supporting Never Trust The One You Love and continuing to support the rest of The Hot Boyz series. We truly love and appreciate you all.

CONTENTS

v

ACKNOWLEDGMENTS

First and for most I would like to thank the almighty GOD for giving me this gift to be able to use my creativity to write an awesome book! I also want to thank my best friend T.L Joy who opened up this door for me to write books, I'm so grateful to have a friend like you! I would like to dedicate this book to my son Samier who has brought so much meaning to my life. I truly believe without him that I wouldn't have even made it this far in life. I also will like to acknowledge my loving father, mother, grandmamma, and the rest of the Wiley and Krisel family who have always been there for me, pushing me to achieve all my goals and dreams! And most of all thank you to all the fans of the HOT BOYZ SERIES!!!!!

-Simone Majors

Book cover Designed by: Kellie Dennis from Book Cover By Design

Published by Mahogany Publications

www.mahoganypublications.com

<u>Simone</u>

2011

It was all over with. The deed was done. No more lies, no more betrayal, no more Hot Boyz, no more gangs, and no more of this fucked up lifestyle for me. When I killed Jake, I killed it all. As I sped down the highway, I felt a new freedom. Things were about to change. I grabbed my phone and dialed Sweetz's number.

"It's all done girl. It's all done!" I gloated. "No!" She shrieked. "They're fuckin' onto us Simone! They're on to us!" She yelled frantically. "What the fuck do you mean that they're onto us?" I asked confused. "They're on to us!" She repeated loudly this time, like that's supposed to help me know who she is talking about.

"Jake and Jayden is dead, so who the fuck is on

to us?" I asked. "They took the fuckin' kids. They took our fuckin kids!" She cried, causing my heart to sink. "Sweetz who the fuck took our kids? How the fuck could they have taken our kids?" I yelled angrily. "They're on to us Simone..." She sobbed like a baby.

I couldn't take Krazy shit. She wasn't telling me shit that I needed to hear. I placed the phone on speakerphone and dropped it in the passenger seat. "If you don't tell me who the fuck..." I started to go off, but was cut off by the loud sound of police sirens behind me.

I looked up through my rearview mirror, only to see a flock of police cars speeding behind me. I couldn't speed off and flee like I wanted to, because these damn black Audi's were in my way, driving slow as hell. Fuck! How could I have gotten caught? We had this shit planned out perfectly.

As soon as I pulled over, the two black Audi's

sped off with a quickness. "They're on to us." The voice of Sweetz traveled through my mind, and suddenly it clicked. This was a fuckin' set-up! Everything this whole time was a fuckin' set-up!

6 months later

"You have a visitor Ms. Simmons." The guard said as he unlocked my prison cell door.

I slowly turned around, looking at him like he had lost his mind. I haven't had a visitor since they put me in this bitch. I stood up as the guard placed the shackles around my wrists and waist. I hated this feeling of being locked up. I came from living the life of luxury to now living the life of a prisoner. Constraints have never been my friend, I've always been the one to break the rules made by others and play by my own. Instead of playing the game outside the system, I now learned how to play the game within the system to survive. All of this because of what I thought was love. The first man I ever loved betrayed me, even my damn husband! Fuck that thing called loved, cause all that shit ever did for me was get me locked up in this shithole.

"Keep walking 0427" said the guard, as he pushed me out of my thoughts as well as my cell. I followed him into the visitation room where small children and their mothers sat with other inmates. The sight of these small children caused me to think about my missing son. The mere thought of my son being held captive somewhere in this country caused my stomach to churn, and my blood to boil. Thoughts of how I was going to get my son back filled my head as he led me to a table where a mysterious woman sat. With a scarf wrapped around her head, and large black tinted sunglasses on, I sat down studying this woman's face, trying to figure out who the hell was this bitch. But as soon as she opened her mouth, I instantly knew who she was.

"Oh my gosh Simone! I'm so shocked to see you in here" She exclaimed, as I quickly rolled my eyes. Why in the hell, out of all people, Cashmere had to be the one to come visit me? "Shit you ain't the only one who's shocked, how da' hell did you find out I was in here?" I said with a raised brow. "Well it's kind of hard not to know you're in here. Girl you're on every news station throughout L.A!" She smiled with that devilish smirk of hers.

"Yeah, I guess you're right, but what is the point of you coming to see me? You're are acting like we are cool or something. When you know good and well we had our differences." I glared into her dark tinted sunglasses. She slowly sat back in her chair while taking off her sunglasses, revealing her now grey contacts. Digging into her purse, she pulled out a crinkled piece of paper and slid it across the table.

"Well I thought I should give you this." She said calmly, as I quickly picked up the paper. "What the hell is this?" I asked out loud. My eyes instantly connected to the picture on the front when I realized what it was. "I tried to contact you but, every time I called your phone it was saying something like it was disconnected. Then I clicked on the TV and found out that you were in here. So I figured that it was only right to tell you". Cashmere said innocently, as I slammed the piece of paper back down on the table. With a single tear rolling down my face, I looked at the picture of Kris in his suit on the front page, the same picture we took at Mike's funeral. More tears started to form when I realized that I was cropped out of the damn picture!

"What happen to him? Who did this to Kris?" I nearly choked on his name. "Well you should know you were that last one that talked to him." She said sarcastically, causing me to wipe the tears from my eyes, and glare at her with pure hatred. "Last time I talked to him was before Jake passed. So how would I know anything that was going on with him?" I spat. She looked me up and down before letting out a little fake ass laugh. "Well the word around town was that he was running his mouth so people in higher places decided to silence him."

At that moment, I instantly became enraged. "What the hell you mean people in higher places? Kris never had any beef with anybody, let alone anyone in no damn higher places!" Cashmere took a deep breath before replying "Well obviously he did if he got shot up in an alley back in Cali." My heart sunk thinking who would do this to Kris. Out of all people why him? Cashmere studied my face like she was somehow reading my mind as she went on with the story.

"Yeah they said it was well over fifty rounds

found in his body and pronounced him dead right there at the scene. Shit..." She paused and let out a little chuckle. "They didn't even bother taking him to the hospital; they took that ass straight to the morgue. It was even worst that no one came to the funeral, everyone at least thought that you would have been there."

I looked at her in disgust "And where was you when this all happened? Wasn't ya'll cool, or maybe that ain't the right term to use to describe ya'll...hmmm I should say fuck buddies or maybe you were just his hoe." I said, hitting below the belt. Cashmere smacked her lips with annoyance before slowly replying. "I had business to handle elsewhere." Now that really tickled me when that bitch said that, she know damn well she didn't have any damn business to handle. "Yeah, aiight." I laughed, as I leaned back in my seat.

"Speaking of business to handle, I heard you're missing your son...such a damn shame huh? My momma always told me that when it rain it pours. You get locked up for killing your man, and you lose your son in the process, what a mess!" She continued, getting under my skin. "I don't appreciate you coming up here talkin' shit like this." I said, trying to remain calm before I knocked this chick out. "Oh no honey...I'm not here to talk shit, I'm just here to inform you." "You already informed me about Kris, so what else is there to inform me about?" I asked with an attitude.

"Oh it's a lot I could inform you about, but I don't plan on being here long since I have business to handle. So I'm just going to keep this visit short and sweet." Cashmere said with a smirk, as she began to gather her belongings. "Whatever Cashmere." I rolled my eyes, blowing her ass off. "Hmm, have you talked to your girl Sweetz lately?" She asked as she stood up. "If not, then I think it's best to give her a call, and see how that search for your baby is going." Cashmere stated as she walked away, leaving me steaming mad.

How the hell did she know about me and Sweetz? Is this what Sweetz meant when she said that they're onto us? That was also the last time I ever heard from Sweetz. I never bothered to call her since I assumed that she was busy searching for the kids, and that she would come see me when she had more information.

Better yet, how would Cashmere know about the kids being missing? Is Cash a part of this whole setup? Yeah, she had to be... How else would she have known about me talking to Kris before he died and about the kids missing? I need to call Sweetz. I hate to admit it, but Cashmere was onto something. I have to get to the bottom of this shit.

I couldn't wait until my phone time arrived, I immediately dialed Sweetz's number anticipating to hear her answer the phone, and give me the lowdown about this shit that's going on in the real world. Yet I was greeted by the operator telling me that the number I dialed was no longer in service. What the fuck? I hung up and dialed again, not giving a fuck about the other inmates and their bullshit. Once again, I was greeted with the same automated reply about her number not being in service. I couldn't understand this shit; Sweetz had the same cell phone number since we were fuckin' fifteen! I knew damn well she wouldn't just change her number on me like that...Or would she?

As I laid in my jail cell, so many thoughts protruded in my head. Although I acted like I didn't have a clue about Kris getting killed off by "people in higher places" as Cashmere would put it; I knew good and well what happened. Someone had to have set him up and killed him; the real question is "Who?" Who set up and killed Kris, and why? I know Jake and Jayden didn't do it cause I know for damn sure Kris would have killed them, before they killed him...So who was it? "There are eyes everywhere baby. I don't care what state you move to, there are eyes everywhere." The voice of Kris lingered in my head, and that's when I knew... It had to be Smooth...

<u>Smooth</u>

I watched as Sweetz laid in the bed, sleeping peacefully. Her long, wavy black hair scattered all over the pillows, as her brown angelic face glowed under the dimly lit light. Too bad the transition to get her here wasn't as sweet as her namesake. As I sat on the edge of the bed, sparking a Cuban cigar, thoughts of eight months ago quickly began to flood through my mind.

Flashback:

"What the hell is going on?" Sweetz fumed, as she hopped out of her car and walked up to me as I stood outside the vacant warehouse. "You already know what it is." I simply stated. "No!" She yelled. "You left me pregnant and alone over all those years. And now you come back with this bullshit." Sweetz continued as she slapped me across the face.

There was no point in fighting or arguing with her, because I already had the upper hand. I had what she wanted in my possession, something she couldn't leave without… the kids. I had my two workers, Liyah and Cashmere, take them right from under her nose. While she was in the gas station getting distracted, they moved in and slid the kids right from under her nose. The only way to get

Sweetz back in my presence was to take away the very thing that she loves dearly.

"That wasn't a part of the plan Smooth!" She yelled, finally catching my attention. Doesn't take long for me to tune her out when she is rambling on and on. I smiled in response, "Sweetz, Sweetz Sweetz... My pretty ass Sweetz." I gently caressed her face until she quickly smacked my hand away. "Haven't I always told you that nothing ever goes as planned? Shit happens baby girl, so you better learn how to roll with the punches from now on." I explained. "Or what?" She said with an attitude, as she folded her arms and looked me up and down.

Sweetz always knew I wasn't the one to be fucked with, but maybe our time apart caused her to gain amnesia. Without hesitation, I punched her in the face, causing her to collapse on the ground with blood flowing from her nose and mouth. "Or else next time your hoe ass will be lying on this ground with a bullet in your head." I spat foully, quickly reminding her that the old Smooth was back, and all that old lovey dovey shit was thrown out the window. She held her bleeding nose, while she looked up at me in disbelief. Yet I didn't give a fuck how she felt.

At this point in time, the love I had for Sweetz was on hold, and we were now strictly business. "Now get your ass up and let Liyah take you inside to clean your ass up. We got business we need to get back to, and I don't have time to fool with your bullshit. You got that." I commanded, while I grabbed her up by the collar of her blouse and held her up to my face. Tears flooded out her eyes as she nodded her head in agreement. "Good." I smiled, as I dropped her, allowing her to once again fall back onto the ground. My little sister Liyah rushed over to Sweetz to help her up off the ground.

As I began to walk away, I heard Sweetz crying and whimpering behind me yet the monster that I've became wouldn't allow me to feel any sympathy for her. Instead, all I could think was "Mirror, Mirror, on the wall I 'am my father after all."

An hour later Sweetz finally joined me in my office that I created within this low-key warehouse. She was no longer in blood stained attire, but now was dressed in clean clothes and feeling much better after taking a capsule of molly, which was the purest form of MDMA , or known as ecstasy to all. I knew that would get her right where I needed her. Since I needed her to be calm, one was enough for now, but later on when she starts acting up I have a large supply to keep her how I want her. "So wassup?" She smiled as she sat down in front of my desk.

"Business as usual." I replied calmly. "Little Mi'quel and Jake are here, but in order for you to see

them you have to play by my rules" I explained.
"What are the rules?" She asked. "You are mine
now. You will be living with me, helping me build my
new business venture and taking care of the kids.
Living in Cali and Detroit is out... We have to
relocate and start fresh." I began.

"—But what about the Hot Boyz?" She asked.
"Ain't no more Hot Boyz. That shit died when Mike
got put six feet under." I fumed, feeling my blood boil
at the thought of the Hot Boyz. "There will be no
more gang shit, and we won't be selling like we use
to. Only enough to help get my business where it
needs to be. I will have steady clients that you will
help distribute our products to. You just do what I
say and if you play your cards right this time, I will
give you whatever you want. Just like the old times.
You got that?" I explained. Sweetz smiled at the
thought of the old times. "Yes." She answered.
"That's my girl. " I smiled back at her. "I really

missed you baby." She blurted out. "Oh yeah… well come here." I instructed her. Without hesitation Sweetz made her way over to me. "What do you want me to do baby?" She asked innocently. Although I only see her as business right now, there is nothing wrong with a little bit of pleasure.

"Do what you know pleases me." I commanded, before she dropped down to her knees and pleased me the right way. From that moment on, I knew that as long I kept her under my "drug spell," she would continue to abide by my rules.

<u>Sweetz</u>

I laid in the master bedroom, staring at him. I couldn't move, I couldn't even talk, and all I could do was stare. "You straight?" He asked me, yet it all was slow and slurred. Everything was spinning, and my head was throbbing in pain. "Yeaaaaah, I'm ok." I replied, as I wiped my nose with the white, powdery substance still on my hand.

"I know you was uptight earlier...but you feel good don't you babe?" He smiled, as he rubbed my arm. I looked up into his honey colored eyes, not knowing what to say. "Yeah, you don't even have to tell me. I can look at yo' ass and know that you are feeling good. So good you might be up to make baby number two huh?" Smooth chuckled. As soon as he said the word baby, the thought of Mi'quel and little Jake triggered in my head. Where are they?

"The kids..." I muttered. "Yeah what about them? Do you remember when we dropped them off at Liyah's?" Smooth asked, as I looked at him blankly. "We are going to let them stay at Liyah's for a while, so we can get some quality time. Trust me, they are in good hands." Smooth reassured. "We did this for us remember? We always wanted to have that family of our dreams. You, me, and our three kids... Raise them like how I always wanted me, Liyah and Mike to be raised." Smooth gleamed.

"Now that we have Jake and Mi'quel...We just have to make a little girl." He continued. But all I heard come out of his mouth was "little girl". A little girl that I once had dreams about, a little girl that I knew I was supposed to give birth to, and the little girl that I gave away. I had to end the life of my little girl, all because of her! That stupid bitch, who didn't even have a clue about the love Kris and I shared. What made her so fuckin' special that I had to give away my child at the abortion clinic?

I remember when I first met Kris. I was fifteen living in the house that Smooth provided for us. I had to hold it down at home, while Smooth tried to get the Hot Boyz gang up and running. Dressed in my little wife beater and pink shorts, I sat on the couch watching TV when Smooth walked in with this mysterious boy. He was tall and chocolate, with grey eyes and long braids. I could see the tattoos covering his body under his black wife beater, and I could tell he was hardcore compared to Smooth.

"Sweetz, this is Kris and Kris this is Sweetz...I need to go down the street and get some shit from Pistol so you guys just stay here for a min, I'll be back." Smooth said abruptly, and left us before we could even say a word.

Kris stood there and stared at me as I stared back at him. Our eyes locked and I could feel the tingles shoot down my spine. "Damn ma', how can your man just leave you alone with me like that?" He said lowly. "I mean, I guess he has a lot of trust in you." I shrugged as he sat next to me. "If I was him, I wouldn't trust me…Especially with a pretty girl like you." He said, causing me to giggle.

"You got such a pretty smile, and such a cute laugh." He complimented. "Thank you." I replied nervously. Smooth never complimented me like this. He barely had time to even recognize the little things about me since he was so busy on the streets. I shyly looked up at him, only to see him staring at me like he was ready to pounce on me. I instantly got turned on when he licked his lips at me and eyed my body up and down. The sexual tension was thick, and I couldn't take it.

With one aggressive movement, I leaned in, grabbed his face, and began kissing him. His lips *were so soft, and I loved how he traced my face and body with his hands as we kissed. I grabbed at his manhood through his jeans, and continued to share our first kiss. He was so passionate and gentle with me; as I was so aggressive and wild with him and I loved it. The sound of keys jingling outside the front door caused us to break the kiss. "I'm back!" Smooth announced, as he walked through the door. Luckily Kris and I were on opposite ends of the couch, playing it off like nothing just happened. Smooth didn't have a clue about us, and that turned me on even more.* After that very moment, Kris captured my heart and we became what I thought was the definition of "lovers."*

"Come here." Smooth commanded, snapping me out of my thoughts of Kris and I. I looked over at Smooth sitting in his chair by the bed. *"Don't do it!"* The twisted voice said behind me. I turned around to see who said it, but there was no one there. "Don't play games Sweetz, come here girl." He said. *"No, don't go."* The voice said again. "Leave me alone!" I screamed, looking back at the wall again. "Sweetz, what the fuck is going on with you? That shit got you trippin huh?" Smooth snapped, as he stood up and headed over to me. *"Run."* The voice commanded. Hopping out the bed, I ran out the room, and made my way down the hall.

"Keep running…Get out of here Sweetz." The voice commanded, as I ran faster. Smooth chased after me, but that wasn't stopping me. I grabbed the vase off a nearby table and threw it at him to slow him down. "What the fuck!" He yelled out. I made my way to the top of the stairs when I slipped and fell down the first flight of stairs. Reaching the platform on top of the second flight of stairs, I ended up flat on my stomach.

"Go away!" I screamed at the voices in my head

as I sat up, and banged my head against the wall. I balled up into the fetal position, feeling the agonizing pain in both my head and my stomach. The pain in my stomach brought back horrible memories of that horrible day when Kris made me give away my baby. Cradling my stomach, tears started to flow down my face as the visions of me and Kris at the clinic replayed in my head.

Smooth ran down the steps, gathering me into his arms, and started to wipe the tears from my eyes. I studied his face as it went from rage to concern. "Sweetz baby, what's going on with you? I thought that this is what you wanted." I sniffled and look at him deep into his eyes "I want to see Mi'quel." I said barely above a whisper. Smooth looked at me with deep concern in his eyes, "Whateva' you want Sweetz, we're going to go pick him up from Liyah's house and bring him back here with us." "And Lil Jake too?" I asked. "Yes baby, him as well." He replied, before carrying me back into the bedroom.

"You need to get some rest babe, sleep this shit off ok?" Smooth suggested, as he laid me down on the bed. "It's hard babe when I hear all these voices in my head." I replied. "Voices?" Smooth stood there with a raised eyebrow. "Baby what you mean by voices?" He asked.

"They keep talking to me...telling me to do things." I said softly. "Girl, that shit is just getting to your head. I think you need to lay off the lines for a while. Especially if we are getting the kids back, I'mma need you to be alert and in your right mind." Smooth said, as he began to lie next to me on the bed. "Ok." I sighed, before giving up on this conversation. This wasn't the first time I've been hearing voices in my head, but maybe Smooth was right it could be the drugs, or maybe I'm really going crazy.

I woke up the next morning, alone in the bed. I needed that rest to help me get over the effect that this coke had on me. I rolled over, only to find myself alone in the bed. Yet the sound of running water coming from the bathroom reminded me that it was time to have a little "shower time" with my sexy love.

As I peeled out of my clothes, I looked over and admired the sight of Smooth under the shower head. His muscles were sculpted to perfection; biceps, triceps, and that sexy v-cut. No one could deny that Smooth had the body of an Adonis. His tattoos on his neck, arms, chest, and back were so appeasing against his caramel skin. It's been awhile since I actually had a good look at him, since I was always under the influence. I know Smooth put me through so much shit in the past, but every time I looked at him, it seems as if I would fall in love with him all over again.

"You comin' in or what?" Smooth asked, as he popped his head out of the shower. "Yes baby, here I come..." I replied, as I walked over to him in my birthday suit. He couldn't take his eyes off me as he licked his lips. As soon as I stepped into the shower, I grabbed him by the back of his head, and kissed him passionately. "I love you Smooth." I said as I pulled away from the kiss, and bent over and touched my toes. The warm water rolled down my back, as I made my ass cheeks clap for him. "Now come get this daddy." I commanded in a sexy voice. "Mmm...Damn I love you more girl!" Smooth exclaimed, before taking my warm, wet, and inviting access pass.

<u>Smooth</u>

After a hot 'n' steamy session in the shower, it was time to get dressed and head to my sister Liyah's house in Staten Island. Both dressed in our leather bomber jackets, v-cut white tees, jeans, his and her aviator shades, and Gucci shoes for me and stilettos for her; we were both looking fly. "The hottest couple in New York" was what they called us. After the fall of the Hot Boyz, I moved to New York and started a new life. I went from running a gang, to running a lucrative sports agency business. Just one endorsement with one of my top athlete's and I can easily make $400 million per deal.

I've worked with the best athletes in the game and racked up on my net worth to the point that I don't even have a desire to be affiliated with a gang ever again. I'm on top of my game, even though I had to do some shady shit to get to this point, sometimes you have to make sacrifices in order to get to where you want to be. And nothing could be better than to be sitting behind the driver's seat of the latest Aston Martin Luxury car, with my sexy Sweetz by my side. I chuckled to myself as Kanye West explained to me how no one man should have all that "Power" from my stereo, and I couldn't agree with him more. The shit a man has to do to obtain power is animalistic and purely foul, but I swear power and wealth looks so damn good on me.

"Do you want me to go in with you?" Sweetz asked as we pulled up in front of my sister's house. "Naw, you just stay right here and look pretty." I said, while flashing her my charming smile. She couldn't help but giggle in response. "Ok baby, but don't take too long, it's cold out here." "Girl you got the heat on. You will be aiight." I replied, before hopping out of the car, and heading towards the front door. Since I called my sister Liyah to let her know I was coming ahead of time, she left the door unlocked for me.

"I don't have all day so let's try to make this quick." I said as I walked into the living room, only to see Liyah sitting on the edge of the couch with her head down. "What's going on?" I asked, as I looked around. I didn't see any signs of anyone else here, not even one noise from a child. "They're gone." She mumbled. "What? Who's gone?" I responded. Liyah looked up at me with tear filled eyes before she answered, "The kids are gone." "What do you mean the kids are gone?" I interrogated, trying to keep my composure. "After you called, I let little Mike and Jake go outside to play like I usually do. I went back inside to make a phone call about some business, and when I got done, I went back outside and they were gone." Liyah explained, but I wasn't hearing it.

"What the fuck do you mean that they are gone

Liyah?" I yelled, as I backhanded her out of rage.
"This is fucking Staten Island, and they are the only
two black kids on the block, don't nobody want two
little black boys out here, so what the fuck do you
mean they are gone?" I continued. "I don't know,
when I came back outside they were gone." Liyah
replied in-between sobs. "Why the fuck did you leave
them outside by themselves anyway? These are two
year old boys, not some fucking pit bull puppies you
found off the street! What the fuck is wrong with you
Liyah?" I yelled, as I smacked her again. "I-I don't
know." Liyah cried, causing my blood to boil even
more at her stupidity.

"Well let me remind your dumb ass." I replied, as
I grabbed her up by the collar of her wife beater, and
threw her up against the wall. "You fucked up Liyah,
you really fucked up!" I spat full of anger. "I know, I
know..." She cried harder. "No, you stop all that
fuckin' crying." I slapped her across the face. "You

fucked up big time, this isn't money or drugs we are talking about, this is my fuckin son we are talking about. Do you understand the difference?" "Uh-huh" She nodded. "I don't think you do, so let me remind you." I retorted, as I held her by the neck with one hand and pistol whipped her with my glock.

All I could see was the thought of my son being kidnapped by some strangers, as I threw her down on the ground, and began punching and kicking the shit out of her. I didn't give a flying fuck if this was my blood sister or not, and I for damn sure didn't care at the fact that I'm beating a female; as manly and as tough this dyke is, beating her was equivalent to beating a fucking man off the street. Liyah had fucked up big time, and I wanted to make it clear to her just how much she had fucked up. By the time I got done beating that ass, Liyah had a busted lip, dislocated jaw, broken nose and a bruised rib cage to show just what happens when you fucked up with a nigga like me.

"Now you find them fuckin' kids, or I'm going to come back and take care of you for good, you hear me?" I commanded, as I stood over her weak body lying on the floor. "Y-y-" She muttered with a mouth full of blood. "Speak up bitch!" I said foully, as I kicked her again in the stomach. "Yes!" She yelled out in pain. "Good, now go clean yourself up and go find them fuckin kids." I replied, as I stared at her in disgust one last time before I headed out the front door. I tucked my gun safely back in its holster and placed my leather gloves over my bloody knuckles before hopping back into the car with Sweetz.

"What's goin' on? Where are the kids?" Sweetz interrogated. Damn, I hated to have to do this to her again. "They're gone." I said lowly, as I started up the car and pulled out of the driveway. "Gone? Like dead?" She panicked. "No, they aren't dead... I hope not, but they are missing." I answered calmly. I couldn't allow Sweetz to see my real emotions towards this situation, because I knew she would lose it. "Missing? How the hell are they missing when they were with Liyah? That doesn't make any sense Smooth." She started. I sighed heavily as I explained to her what happened. I knew this was going to be an all day thing, I would never hear the end of this.

"I-I –I can't believe this. I haven't seen my baby in months and now he is missing? And little Jake too? I just can't… I can't…" She paused and started to cry like a baby. "C'mon Sweetz, hold it together, at least wait 'til we get home and do all that cryin' shit." I reasoned to her. "Wait 'til we get home? What the fuck? My fucking son and little Jake are missing. I lost everything I ever fucking had and you want me to wait 'til I get home? Are you serious right now?" She continued to go on and on through her cries, but I wasn't hearing it. I had too much shit on the brain to even care what she was saying, I cut the music back on and replayed Kanye West's "Power" on our way back home. I guess he was right, no one man can have all this power... especially if the price you have to pay, could place the safety of everyone you love at a dangerous risk.

<u>Introducing Liyah</u>

I struggled to get up out of the pool of my own blood, and headed over to my cell phone on the kitchen counter. I dialed my partner's number and greeted her with an immediate "Help." "I'm on my way!" She responded urgently. Within ten minutes Cashmere was right at my side, helping me make my way out of the house, and into to the car. "I can't believe Smooth did that you!" She exclaimed in shock as we zoomed down the street, heading towards the local hospital.

"I knew he was going to blow up when you told him, but not like this." She continued. "Yeah," I replied weakly. "You know how Smooth likes to make an example out of you when you fuck him over." I continued. "Hmm, I guess." Cashmere chimed full of attitude. I knew Cashmere wanted to turn around and go beat Smooth's ass one good time, it was in her nature to protect the one she loved. I was not just "business partners" with Cashmere; I was her lover and had been her main lover for as long as I could remember. No man or woman could come between us. We were the true definition of lovers and friends. Cashmere was my ride or die, and very loyal to me, as I 'am to her. There is nothing better in this world than a woman's loyalty. When you fuck up and lose a woman's loyalty, you basically just fucked up and lost the world.

My thoughts were quickly interrupted when we arrived to the local hospital. As soon as I stepped into the entrance, one look at my bruised and bloody face, and I instantly received medical care. I wasn't lying about Smooth making an example out of me. With twelve stitches, a closed up eye, broken nose, a dislocated jaw, and a fucked up ribcage, Smooth definitely made his point. Yet I was a firm believer in Karma, and just how I like the taste of my women against my tongue, is how I like the taste of my revenge... I like it served sweet.

<u>Simone</u>

Tears cascaded down my cheeks as I laid in my bunk bed of my jail cell. I still can't believe Kris was gone. The only best friend I had since I first learned to talk, my first love, my only family, and my partner in this crazy gang world was gone. Shit wasn't perfect between us. We had our good and bad times. Who doesn't in this thing called love? I hated the fact that Kris and I had to end the way we did. Looking back at it, I could've changed our outcome when I had the chance. All Kris wanted was to get out of the gang life and start a new and clean life. Damn, why did I have to be so stubborn and full of anger towards him? Even though he made me go through hell and back in the past, I still loved and appreciated everything he did for me. I just wish I could've told him that while he was alive.

As I laid in my bed mourning over Kris, I couldn't help but hear the shrieking screams of the girl in the next cell. I could see the shadows of females within the cell grouped around her, ravishingly inflicting pain on her.

The next morning I was awaken by the guards frantically rushing down the cell block. I sat up in my bunk as they pulled out the body of a young black girl who was mutilated. As they dragged her body past my cell I instantly jump out the bunk bed and threw up in the toilet from the sight and the stench of the body. This shit is real and me sitting in this cell crying day in and day out is going to get me killed! At that moment I realized that I had to do whatever I need to do to survive and the only way of doing that was to learn the ins and outs of surviving in prison.

Over time, I sat back and observed everything and everyone in this prison. I learned who was who and what a person would have to do to survive. With that in mind, I created a plan to survive in this bitch and to do what I had to do to recruit some bitches on my team. All my life I was the one getting my hands dirty while Smooth and Kris sat on their "throne" like they knew about putting in work! I looked around the prison day in and day out during my free time, I knew I had to make my name be known and I had to do it fast. And the best way to do that was to get the grittiest bitches to even respect and follow me.

Now everyone always thinks you have to take down the biggest bitch in prison to gain respect when that isn't the case. You have to find the one with the biggest pull on the inside and on the outside, and word of mouth was that the one in charge was my good ol' friend Samya. Over time, I found out that she was over in C- block serving time for heavy distribution of narcotics. As I suspected, her weak ass was sitting pretty on the lowest level of the prison, while I'm up here in D-block, fighting for my damn life every fuckin' day and night from these murdering coochie snatching bitches! Luckily for me, half of these chicks here in D- block are serving 25 to life, or are even on death row, so my plan was to cater to their needs which was supplying "coochie". In order to do that, all I had to do was get the baddest bitch on my team, which turned out to be my cellmate Hannah aka Blondie.

Blondie stood at 5'2 with long bleach platinum blonde hair that fell down to her ass. For her being a white girl you knew she was paid because she had to have the best plastic surgeon that constructed that Barbie like facial structure. She had a coke bottle shape that would put Ice-T's wife Coco to shame! Every lesbian woman desired to have Blondie all to themselves, which is why I needed to have her on my team. After four days of her being in the pen, I decided to make a move. It was time for me to get her to recognize my power and seek me out for love and protection.

"Aye yo' Blondie, you good over there?" I asked while she sat on her bunk bed crying. "Yeah, I'm sorry if I'm keeping you up; I just can't believe they gave me 25 years for killing that bastard! He's the one who put his hands on me! I didn't mean to kill him!" She muttered out in between sobs. "Don't worry about all that. " I started as I sat up in my bunk bed. "You are going to be good as long as you're in here with me. Ain't no bitch about to fuck with you." I reassured her.

"Are you sure? I'm not trying to start nothing, but you don't look like the type that would intimidate anyone." Blondie replied, causing me to laugh in response. "You might think that now 'cause I'm not trying to let you see that side of me. But where I'm from, I'm well known in the streets. People damn near pissed on themselves from hearing my name. But right now I'm just playing it cool, trying to do my bid." I explained.

"Wow, you sound so confident that no one is going to test you." She said with amazement. "Shit they might, but I ain't worried 'bout it cause as soon as they do, I'mma send them to their maker. Either way, it's not like it's going to change anything...Shit a bitch in here twenty-five to life without a possibility of parole so fuck it!" I exclaimed.

"Damn, well I don't want to bother you with my issues...that's like putting an extra load on you." Blondie replied.

I got off my top bunk, and stood in front of Blondie. I looked at her deeply in her blue eyes before speaking. "Don't even worry about all that cause I can tell that you ain't got one lick of street smarts in you and all these bitches are going to hop on you like a bitch in heat. But I got you 'til the wheels fall off my baby, so don't fret your pretty little head about any situation. If you ever get scared, or if anyone is fucking with you just come and let me know ok?" I said sweetly before kissing her on the side of her cheek. At that moment, my plan came into full effect.

From that day forward, I made Blondie stay close to me. I hardly let her go out the cell alone because I know bitches be waiting and checking for any moment she was alone. Bitches in here are just like niggas when a bad bitch is by herself any nigga would try to get on. Since today was laundry day, it was the perfect opportunity to execute my plan.

I sat in the TV room with the other inmates watching the news while Blondie went into the laundry center. I positioned myself in a way where I could see her washing clothes when Big Anna Mae and her clique walked in. The fear on Blondie face let me know that they weren't there on a friendly note. Our clothes flew across the floor as Big Anna Mae grabbed Blondie and threw her across the folding table and started to rip off her inmate uniform. I slowly stood and walked over to the laundry center while getting my handmade shank out my uniform. I pushed my way into the room and with a running jump I stabbed Big Anna Mae in the neck. Letting go of Blondie she turn her attention to me while putting pressure onto her neck, next thing you know me and five bitches was getting down.

I haven't fought like this in so long, but the adrenaline rushing through my body felt so good it was almost like having an orgasm! When the guards finally came, all who were left standing was me and Big Anna Mae, while the rest of her clique laid on the floor in critical condition. Drops of blood from Big Anna Mae's crew ran down my face as the guards restrained me, Blondie stood there crying hysterically before looking into my eyes and that's when I gave her my all-time winning smirk letting her know that I wasn't fazed. They took me and Big Anna Mae to the hole where I sat there for two months, but once I was out Blondie was all mine.

With one bad bitch on my team and my reputation steady growing, every bad chick that came into D-block got down on my team. Everyone on D-block had to come to me if the wanted to get a taste of one of my bad bitches. With Blondie as my main chick flipping coochie was my new hustle. Ain't shit free up in D-block not even the pussy!

Within the next couple months, I had Big Anna Mae on my team and she even introduced me to this Russian named Anastasia, who had some drug connects on the outside. Now that I assembled my squad, it was time to take Samya out of the game and run the whole L.A. prison system from the inside! My account stayed doing numbers, fuck having connects in the states I had the oversea connects and money. I put everything I learned from years in the game into effect, I manipulated these women just like Kris did them hoes back in Detroit.

If I said a chick owed me money they flipped that back tenfold, and if I felt disrespected, then my team were the first ones to go out and kill the bitch. My reputation was known throughout every cell block, I even had a couple of prison guards on my team on the low. Now that I've created a name for myself, I had to make the next move and take out Samya, who was the next in charge.

The day finally came for Samya to meet her maker, just as I promised years ago! My whole squad sat in the lunchroom as C-block came in with Samya at the front of the line. Samya and I made eye contact when she gave me a smirk testing me to make a move. I leaned over and whispered in Blondie ear letting her know it was her time to prove her worth to the squad. She stood up and walked over to Samya as instructed and began to woo her as a peace offering between our cliques. I watched as they walked back into the kitchen, as I suspected Samya still was naive to the game like always and took Blondie as the "offering." One rule to the game is never fall for pussy and this stupid bitch did just that.

Samya

I knew Krazy would come around and try to get back in my good graces. I was running shit from the inside and had connections from the outside. Who wouldn't want to fuck with me?

Thoughts of me and my takeover came to a sudden halt when I felt the hands of Blondie roaming my body from behind me. I closed my eyes and enjoyed it as she was kissing on me in between whispering nasty gestures in my ear. This girl had game and I was loving it! I moaned from the pleasure I was receiving as her hand was gently chocking my neck like I liked it. Everything was all good until I felt a cold metal blade up against my throat. At that moment I knew that this was one of Krazy's set up and I had fallen right into the trap!

<u>Krazy</u>

I sat at my table waiting to see what was about to go down after Samya and Blondie slid off to the kitchen where the guards couldn't see them. Minutes passed before one of the cooks let out a blood curdling scream, causing the guards to rush back to the kitchen. Only to discover that Blondie had slit Samya's throat as requested from yours truly! Without a tear in her eye Blondie was sent to the hole and I became the top bitch in every block. Bitches cowered in fear just by hearing my name and Krazy was back in full effect!

3 years later

"Get up, and let's go!" The prison guard demanded loudly, waking me out of my slumber. Jumping out of my bunk bed, I made my way out of my jail cell, and stood in line with the other prison inmates. It was lunchtime, and as much as I didn't want to eat that slop that they served us, a bitch was hungry.

I sat at a back table, with my back pressed up against the cement wall, as my squad surrounded me. Even though I was running shit, I still didn't trust these females, and rule number one to stay alive in prison was to never have anyone sitting or standing behind you. I've seen so many bitches getting raped or killed in here as soon as they turned their back. If you leave yourself open and vulnerable, you're basically asking for a death wish. I still kept my guards up; even if everyone here knew that I wasn't the one to be fucked with. As soon as they heard my story of taking over the whole prison system, no one had the balls to come and fuck with me. No one outside my squad even muttered a word to me, and that is exactly how I like it.

"Ayo Krazy!" A voice yelled out at me. I looked up confused, only to see a short, Latina girl with wavy brown hair, pencil thin eyebrows, and what looked like black lip liner tattooed on her full lips, trying to approach me. I studied her up and down in her bright orange prison attire. Her arms were covered with tattoos and on her neck she had a tattoo that read "Skipper." Now what would a girl named Skipper, want to talk to me about? The only thing she can talk to me about is being a new candidate to my stable.

"I just got in this bitch, and word on the block is that we are going to cell-mates yo!" She said energetically in her thick New York accent. "Plus I heard that we both got locked up for the same shit, that's crazy right?" She continued, as she stood in front of me. Anastasia and Big Anna Mae stood close to this newcomer, just to make sure she didn't try anything stupid. All I could do was look at her, and continue to eat my food. This chick was clearly as crazy as I was. I never met someone so excited, and happy to be in prison...until now.

"I see you not much of a talker, but that's ok." She said, as she pushed passed Anastasia and Big Anna Mae and sat across from me; not fazed by their presence. They looked at me ready for the word to pounce on Skipper's little ass, but me being so impressed by how much balls this little girl had, I let that shit slide.

"My man was the quiet kind too. I remember him sitting there in the loveseat, looking at me as I talked his ears off. Just quiet ya' know? I talked to him for hours until the police came and pronounced him dead." She laughed. "Can you believe it, I was so busy talking my ass off, that I forgot I poisoned this mothafucka' for cheating on me with my sista'?" She said, as I looked at her like what the fuck!

"So that's what you're in for." I finally spoke. "Yep!" She smiled proudly. "I gave that mothafucka' seventeen years of my life while he was the kingpin in our area. I cooked 'n' cleaned, dropped off some of his business, did some hits, whatever he wanted... even had his damn baby. And can you believe…" She paused, as her face turned red, and the veins started to pop out of her neck. "Can you believe he had the nerve to fuckin' sleep with my little sista'? The same bitch I took in after her man K-dubb left her, and their baby, broke and living on the corna'. After all the shit I've done for them, they do me like this?" She said, before she began to cry. "Now that bitch has my child and I can't do nothin' about it." She said in between cries. "Not a damn thing!"

I couldn't believe that she was telling me her life story in the first five minutes of us meeting, but as I looked at her sob and cry her eyes out, I realized that she had nothing to lose, just like me. Everything we ever had, our love, our trust, and now our kids were stripped away from us, as we made the decision to kill the men who had betrayed us. Although the satisfaction of revenge is great, losing our children as we are locked up in prison is bitter.

That's the price we had to pay, but is it really worth it?

Skipper talked my ear off as we made it back to the cell; telling me her story about her and her sister being immigrants from Puerto Rico, living in the hood of Harlem, and becoming prostitutes to survive. Tired of their lifestyle in New York, Skipper and her sister ran away to Atlanta and became strippers. Fortunate for Skipper, she met her late fiancé while she was shaking ass at Magic City.

Seeing her new man Blade as her next big meal ticket, Skipper immediately quit stripping and became a Gangsta's Girl. While her sister La'Tanya met a new thug in town named K-dubb who stole her heart, cashed her out, gave her the world, and eventually left her ass high 'n' dry. Leaving her with nothing…not even a pot to piss in. It was a sad story to hear, but I've seen it plenty of times before.

Smooth left Sweetz high 'n' dry after she got pregnant and even Kris left me for four whole years to do business! That's all a part of the deal when you are dealing with gangstas, either you take it or you leave it.

"And even after all of this, 'Tanya is dyking it out!" Skipper exclaimed, as she leaned against the wall next to my bottom bunk. "Is she now?" I replied. "Mmmhmm, she' fuckin' with this one chick who I swear looks like one of those pretty boys. I didn't even know she was a woman. She just looks like one of those handsome men. And get this, 'Tanya isn't just messing with one chick...she's with two. They are in a three-person relationship...That polyamorous shit." She laughed. "Crazy right?" She suggested, as she lightly slapped me on my shoulder.

"Hell yeah, that's some weird ass shit." I agreed,

as I noticed that my picture of Kris was falling off the wall. I began to retape it while Skipper continued to ramble. "Oooooooh my God!" Skipper exclaimed loudly. I turned around and faced her, only to see her face pale like she had seen a ghost.

"What?" I said, confused at her sudden reaction. "I can't believe it!" She replied. "What is wrong?" I asked with a scrunched up face. "How do you know him?" She interrogated. "Who?" I replied full of confusion. "Don't act dumb bitch! You got his picture up on the wall. So how do you know K-Dubb?" She said, as her temper flared. At that moment, everything came crumbling down, K-Dubb was Kris?

<u>Sweetz</u>

"Now tell me more about this Kris character that you talk of." The woman said as she sat across from me in her chair. I laid against the lounge chair and studied my psychiatrist. She was a short, brown skinned and pleasantly plump woman in her early fifties. She wore business casual attire, funky silver jewelry and wore her natural hair in various styles. Something about her sweet smile, soft and caring voice, and motherly aura made me feel safe and at home when I was around her.

Dr. Toya Webber was her name, and I've been seeing her for the past two weeks after Smooth told me that my son was missing, foreal this time. Last time Smooth kidnapped them only to lure me back to him. After he drugged me up, he announced that my son Mi'quel and Krazy's Son Jake were safe under Liyah's supervision. Unfortunately safe was an understatement.

"You want to know more about Kris?" I asked nervously. "Yes dear, you can pick up where you left off last time, about how you guys met and you instantly became lovers. What happened after that? And did Smooth ever suspect it?" "No...Smooth never knew about us. He was too busy to care or notice anything when it came to me..." I started, as I reminisced about my sacred past.

Smooth never noticed anything that I did. I would change my hairstyles, dress sexier for him, and he would never even compliment me. Not once! I was overlooked and never heard. Every time I would even utter a word to Smooth he would tell me "Shut up and leave me alone. I got business to handle." Business for him to handle would last several days or weeks at the Hot Boyz mansion, at which I was not allowed to visit. Yet, all the time Smooth spent at the Hot Boyz mansion, Kris would be right by my side. Whispering in my ear about how sexy I look, that he loved my hair, and that he was ready to fuck me right there on the spot.

Of course, knowing Kris being so sweet and gentle, I would be the aggressive one out of us two, and I would pull of his clothes and we would fuck right on the living room floor. Not giving a damn if Smooth would happen to come home early and catch us in the act. We would see each other every day and night, constantly making love all over the house. Yet we both knew that if Smooth, and Krazy, my best friend who was dating Kris; were to find out, we would be killed on the spot. It was a dangerous affair, but the thrill and the adrenaline rush of getting caught turned me on so much.

One time, Kris took me over to his place while Krazy was at school, and we fucked in their bed! I *felt like the queen of the world, fucking in the bed that he and her shared. My juices were flowing everywhere, marking my territory all over her bed. Kris was mine, and I didn't give a damn what nobody would say about us. Kris loved me and I loved the fact I was going to have his baby.*

Bursts of joy shot through my body as I stared at the pregnancy test. I've been having dreams lately of holding a little girl in my arms, so I knew I would be having a girl. I immediately called Kris and told him the good news, but he wasn't feeling the same.

"What the fuck do you think this is? A fuckin soap opera?" He yelled as he paced back and forward. I sat on the couch in tears at his response. "I thought you would be happy about this." I cried. "Happy? What type of shit do you think this is? If Smooth ever found out about us he would kill us on the spot! Then Krazy would burn our dead bodies on

fire just for the hell of it! You got life fucked up if you think I'm happy about you getting pregnant. There is no way in hell you are having this baby. We are going to take care of this for once and for all!" He demanded, and that's exactly what we did.

As soon as Kris and I walked into the clinic, I was greeted with the gut wrenching smell of blood and piss. I looked around in disbelief and disgust...How can he just take me to this low down abortion clinic? I continued to look around as we took a seat in the crowded lobby, filled with young girls and a few older women who were worse off than me. Some were three months and way overdue for an abortion, yet they were sitting here in this waiting room with swollen ankles and all.

We sat there for a few more minutes when a nurse came through the big metal double doors calling my name. I was in such a daze that Kris had

63

to pull me out of my seat, and drag me through the doors to the operating room. I didn't want to go, and looking at this place made it even worse. I walked in the operating room only to see rust stained walls, and a long metal table in the middle of the room. I couldn't keep my eyes off the bucket right at the end of the table. Do I really have to go through this? The nurse interrupted my thoughts as she handed me a gown, and a cup. She instructed me to drink the whole cup of numbing medication after I get undressed, and with that said, she made her exit out the room.

I slowly started to roll off my clothes, holding back the tears. "Aye man, make this quick 'cause I gotta' pick Krazy up in a few." Kris demanded, as he sat in the chair texting away on his cell phone. Hearing Krazy's name caused me to instantly get heated. "Man, fuck that bitch! I'm in this doctor office about to have them diggin' all in my shit to kill a baby that is ours." I yelled. "Look man, I already told you the damn deal was…" Kris started, as he stood up. "Now handle this shit, I'mma' be in the car." He finished, before he stormed out of the room.

I couldn't believe how fast Kris went from being my sensitive lover, to a complete, cold-hearted asshole. I finished stripping off my clothes as the tears filled my eyes. I slipped the gown on, and sat on the table looking at the cup before downing it like it was a shot of Remy. As soon as the doctor and nurse came in I started to feel dizzy and numb. They laid me down on the table, and lock my legs in cuffs in order to get ready for the abortion. I flinched when I felt the cold metal forceps enter and I cringed as they jerked around inside of my body. The pain was unbearable! This short amount of time, felt like forever, until finally the nurse said I was finished. I watched as they took the bucket and walk out the room. I sat up feeling lifeless, like a part of me was missing. Well I guess it was, considering it was thrown in a bucket like it had no value.

I held my stomach, even though it was empty with no life within. The nurse came back in and handed me some pads and a piece of paper telling me how to take care of myself after the operation. She helped me put my clothes on, and wheeled me outside to the end of the entrance, where Kris sat in the car on his phone. I sat there weak and not able to move.

"Hurry yo' ass up and get in this damn car!" He yelled. I looked up at him with hate in my eyes, as I clenched on the armrest of the wheelchair. Pulling myself up, and wobbling to the car, I tripped into the door trying to open it, but my hands felt like jello. Finally, I pried the door open and fell into the car. I sat up and grabbed both of my legs, and swung them inside before slamming the door shut. Before I *could even catch my breath from struggling to get into the car, Kris pulled out of the clinic like a mad man. Before I could even mutter a word to him, Kris blasted his music and bobbed his head to the beat, like the shit never happened, and he ignored me as if I was a distant memory in his past.*

"And how do you feel about that La'nay?" Dr. Webber asked, calling me by my first name. "I-I-I…" I stuttered as I tears fell uncontrollably. "I don't know what to feel. I loved Kris…But why? Why would he do that to me?" I said full of pain and confusion. "It seems as though Kris only loved the act of making love, but he's not the type to genuinely love someone." Dr. Webber explained. "Yeah, but the only one he truly loved was that bitch Krazy." I said, cutting her off.

"Not necessarily. He loved her to some extent, but what type of genuine love consists of him betraying her, and sleeping with numerous women including her own best friend? That isn't love La'nay. Kris just thrived off the fact that he can charm women into loving him and doing whatever he asked for. Kris had what I would call a control addiction. He lived, and breathed off of controlling others. It's a shame that you guys were blind to the horrendous mind games he played on you. Made you feel like you are the world to him, and then turned around and made you feel like you were nothing. Like you were nothing but an object that he can use and toss in the garbage." She said, breaking down the real truth to me.

"No one appreciates me." I cried. "I'm just tired of being second to someone else. I know I'm worth more than that, I just wish people would see that." I said sadly, as I looked down at the ground. "You have to let it be known you are worth more. Be bold La'nay and tell the world who you are." Dr. Webber encouraged, but I wasn't accepting that. No one ever listens to me, so why bother. I allowed her to talk and try to uplift my life, as I heard the voices in my head telling me that I'm not worth much.

"Have you been taking your meds lately?" She asked, snapping me out of my trance. "Yeah," I smiled, knowing that I was telling her a bold face lie. "Hmm..." She started, as she gave me that "momma face." "I don't think you are La'nay. How about I prescribe some more and this time we will give them to Smooth. Let him make sure you are taking them. I don't want these voices that you are hearing in your head to get the best of you." She suggested, as I rolled my eyes. Why does everything I do have to be monitored by Smooth? All that shit she was talking, and she is going to turn around and give my independence away to Smooth? Fuck this shit! I'm done with this fake and phony life I'm living. While she was still talking, I grabbed all my shit, and stormed out of the office.

Nicki Minaj's "Save Me" blasted throughout my all white Lexus SUV, as I drove around the city. I feel like I'm all alone in this world. I don't have anyone. The person who I could confide in was Krazy, but now she was gone. Shit, who am I kidding? I never liked the bitch; I hated her down to the bone. Kris fucked me over, and made me give up my baby, for a broad who didn't even want to have his only child. She deserves everything she gets. I hope she rots in jail as they keep her child on ransom.

The loud ringing of my cell phone broke my wicked thoughts of Krazy. "Hello." I answered. "Where are you Sweetz? Smooth has been blowing me up asking me about you!" The voice of Liyah traveled through my phone. "Fuck Smooth!" I yelled out in anger. "I'm tired of this shit. I just need to get away." I said as I began to cry. "I'm tired of living up underneath Smooth's microscope you know?" "I truly understand everything you are saying Sweetz. Having Smooth in your life will always keep you under his control." Liyah said softly. "I'm here if you want to talk. You know I've always been there for you, since day one. Why don't you come over and let Big Daddy take care of you. I've been missing you baby." Liyah suggested in her sexy tone that always turned me on. "Ok," I said as I wiped the tears from my eyes. "I'm on my way." I said, ending the conversation. It was time I do something for me. Do something that pleases me, and tonight I was going to get the best head of my life, from the woman who has been my other secret lover. A huge smile crept on my face as I headed over to Staten Island to see who they call "Big Daddy" a.k.a Liyah.

<u>Simone</u>

My mind hasn't been right after I found out that Kris was K-dubb. The main person who I thought I could really trust betrayed me. It was bad enough that he was sleeping with Cashmere, but to have the nerve to get married and have a child with another bitch for four whole mothafuckin' years is mind boggling! First Jake, now Kris? Why do I have to be the one to get betrayed by the men that I gave my heart to?

"I got some more news to tell you!" Skipper gleamed as the security escorted her back into our cell. "So I talked to my sista' on the phone..." She started, as she sat next to me on my bunk. "So the two girls that she is seeing are named Liyah and Cashmere. They live up in Staten Island now." She explained. "Liyah and Cashmere?" I repeated. "Yup, all in one house with the kids." She continued.

"Whose kids?" I interrogated. "She told me that other than my baby girl and her daughter, 'Tanya has the son of the bitch who has been with K-dubb for years. And guess who that bitch is?" Skipper smiled as she looked at me. "Son of a Bitch!" I yelled out in anger. Liyah and Cashmere set me up this whole time, and I bet they were behind Kris's murder!

Although I could really give two fucks about them killing Kris, especially after the foul shit I found out about him; my blood boiled at the thought of those dyke ass bitches having my son in their home. As soon as I get out of here I'm coming for their asses, and I won't be satisfied until I see blood. How dare they fuck with me, and mine! They must have a death wish, and I'll be there to fulfill it. The only problem is, what plan can I come up with to get out of this bitch?

<u>**Sweetz**</u>

"Mmm, damn you taste so good." Liyah said, as she crawled back up to my face and kissed me on the lips. "It's all yours baby." I replied, as she laid her head on my chest. "It better be!" She demanded, causing us to laugh. "You know I love you girl." Liyah said sweetly as her hands explored my body once again. "I love you too Big Daddy." I replied, calling her by her nickname. It was so peaceful lying in her bed, as I played with her long cornrows that flowed down to the middle of her back. I admired the sexy tattoos that adorned her caramel body that laid on top of mine.

No one knew about the affair Liyah and I shared for over five years. Our affair began back in 2004 when the Hot Boyz gang was in their prime. After I had that forced abortion, Liyah was the only one who I could talk to. She knew everything that went on since she was considered as one of the guys, and Kris had loose lips. Yet she never muttered a word back to Smooth about it. That was one thing I loved about Liyah, she was so loyal and would never turn on you. She could keep your deepest secrets and never judge you. Instead she gave you love and would sit and listen to you which is why her nickname was "Big Daddy."

While Smooth and Kris left to Atlanta, I was left alone at the Hot Boyz mansion for a month with Liyah, and after we shared our first kiss, it was a wrap. We became great lovers and whenever things with Smooth and I weren't working out, she was the one that I would run to.

"I want you to stay with us Sweetz." Liyah suggested, quickly snapping me out of my thoughts. "I mean, we have a family here. You, me, Cashmere, the kids, and La'Tanya. What's better than that?"

She said, as she sat up and smiled at me.
"La'Tanya?" I questioned. "Who is La'Tanya?" I
interrogated, as I quickly sat up in the bed. "She is
our newest edition to the family. She used to be
married to Kris when he was back in Atlanta, and as
you can already predict, he left her ass high 'n' dry.
So I took her in. She is a cool girl Sweetz, you gotta'
meet her and give her some time." Liyah explained.
"I already did enough sharing you with Liyah, but
now you want me to share you with this chick!" I
yelled out in anger. I already hated being placed
under Cashmere, even though our threesomes were
great, I was tired of being Liyah's second lover.

"C'mon Liyah. I love you too much to keep
sharing you." I finished. "I understand that ma', but
just like you and Cashmere, she needs me. She
need's all of us. No one is placed first place, or
second place. I love you all the same and I take care
of all of your needs and wants. We are a family

Sweetz. You know that these niggas ain't shit out here. That's why we females need to stick together and do it right. Take care of home, and raise these babies like they should be raised." Liyah explained, staring at me with those sexy light brown eyes. Damn, I can't resist her. "You're right. We are a family, and we do need to stick together." I finally agreed.

Liyah

I smiled as Sweetz finally gave in. I was always good at persuading bitches, making them do what I ask of them, but these girls were easy. "I'll call La'Tanya up and then you guys can get fully acquainted." I said as I texted 'Tanya and told her to come to my bedroom. Within an instant, 'Tanya made her way to my room on the 4th floor of my house.

She stood there dressed in a sexy black corset and thongs that complimented her light complexion. Rules of the house required every bitch in this house to wear sexy lingerie when the kids were in bed. Standing at 5'5", measuring at 38DD-24-48, 'Tanya was stacked, just like I liked 'em. Her long and wavy, black hair fell down to her ass, as her hazel eyes and vibrating tongue ring made this little Puerto Rican so appeasing to the eye.

"Sweetz, this is 'Tanya. Tanya, this is Sweetz. Now that you know each other's name, how about you guys get fully acquainted the way I like it. I'mma' just sit back and watch." I commanded, as I sat in the chair that was positioned across the bed. I cut on my iPod, and played Usher's Little Freak" with the surround sound; as I sat back, sparked my blunt, and watched the two new lovers in their act.

Once the sexy show was over, it was time for both of them to make me some dinner. They thought we were a "family", but little did these hoes know, they were my own little sex slaves, that does whatever I tell them to. They were brainwashed from day one when they were dealing with those weak ass niggas. All they wanted was love and affection, so I just slid in, told them what they wanted to hear, and now they do it all for me with no questions asked. "Let's shower and get ready to have dinner with the family." I suggested as I headed into the bathroom. 'Tanya and Sweetz followed me like little puppies, and I loved every moment of it. Smooth would be steaming mad if he knew all the things that I had his girl doing on the low.

Simone

"You have a visitor." The prison guard announced as she unlocked my cell. Who the fuck is coming to see me now? If it's that bitch Cashmere, I'm going to shut this bitch down and merk her ass on the spot. I don't care if the guards shoot my ass or not! Crazy thoughts filled my head as I walked to the visitors' room. Yet, as soon as I spotted my old friend from the past, my thoughts quickly faded.

"Pistol, what are you doing here?" I asked as a smile of surprise covered my face. I haven't seen this man in almost four years since I was back in Detroit, living the life associated with Kris and the Hot Boyz gang. Pistol used to be the hit man for the Hot Boyz. He was quick tempered, and also quick to shoot. Still light skinned, bald, and resembling L.L. Cool J, Pistol was now dressed up in an expensive black suit with a royal blue tie, and blinged out cuff links, that probably cost a couple of grand.

"Damn look at you." I smiled as I sat down in front of him. "Look at you girl, you got thicker than a snicker!" He laughed. "Oh stop, you know ain't nothing sexy about being thick in a prison suit." I replied. "I know man, that's why I'm here." He responded with his deep voice. "When the Hot Boyz went under, I moved to New York and got my life right. Went back to college, and then finished out in Harvard Law School. Now I'm a lawyer making powerful moves with powerful people." He explained. "That's nice and all, but, what are you saying?" I interrogated, trying to get to the point. "I'm saying if you stay calm 'n' cool in here and don't cut a bitch, knowing your crazy ass." He chuckled. "I can pull some strings and get you out." Pistol finished. "Is that so?" I said, as I looked at him with a raised eyebrow. "It sure is." He replied.

"And how are you going to do that?" I asked full of curiosity. "Don't worry about that, as much as you did for the Hot Boyz, I owe you. Trust me, I got you." He assured, yet trust has been a hard thing to come by these days. "Hmm, we'll see." I said as I looked at him up and down. Pistol always was a loyal one out of the gang. He always held everybody down and did whatever was needed; I just hope he wasn't on that bullshit like the rest of them.

"You've been all over the news girl; you had CNN and the world talking about what you did to your husband and his brother." Pistol said. "Yeah, I heard." I said nonchalantly. "They charged your ass

for both murders, but we will change that real soon."
He responded with a smile. "You talked to Smooth or
Sweetz lately?" I asked. "Hell no, I don't fuck with
Smooth no more. I heard he's out in New York and
Sweetz lives with him. People talk about them all the
time as being the flyest couple. But that shit is all
fake, you know they are just as fucked up as those
crazies up in the asylum." He laughed. "That bitch
Sweetz is foul." I spat in disgust.

"Yeah, she's not as innocent as you think... Shit
all of the Hot Boyz were fucked up. Liyah, Smooth
and Mike, rest his soul; were all fucked up in the
head, I should know." He chimed in. "What you
mean?" "They are my half-siblings." He announced.
"You were related to them too?" I posed in shock.
"As much as I didn't like it, I was. I was their big
brother, watching over them, until Smooth pulled that
foul ass shit to Liyah." He paused. "What shit?" I
asked, eager to know. "Naw, we will talk about it

later, when I get you out." He replied.

"There is a lot that you need to know." He said, as he leaned back in his seat. "I already know about Kris and his wife 'Tanya." I responded. "How you know about that one?" He jumped up, and leaned in as he held the phone closer to his ear. "I got a bitch in here, her name is Skipper. Crazy little broad, but she is pretty cool. She is the sister of that Tanya bitch and she filled me in on everything. She knew about Liyah and Cashmere having my son and all that. When I get out of here... I swear I'mma..." "Don't say anything else Krazy." Pistol cut me off, as he looked at the guard standing close.

"Like I said, we will talk about it when you get out. There are eyes everywhere so you be on your P's and Q's and let me handle this aiight?" Pistol explained. "Ok." I agreed. "Good. I'll see you soon." He said before he stood up and walked away. I really hope I can trust Pistol to do what he said he would. If he could get me out, that would get me one step closer to seeking my revenge.

<u>Sweetz</u>

"Where the fuck you been?" The voice of Smooth yelled through my phone, as I sat outside on the patio with Liyah and 'Tanya. "Does it matter?" I said with an attitude. "Oh, it's going to matter when I shove my foot up ya'…" He started, but I instantly cut him off. "Look, I don't have time to argue with you. I have things to do today, so I will talk you when I'm ready." I bluntly replied and hung up in his face. It was time I take my life back. I was no longer living under Smooth's microscope. I'm doing things my way.

"I know that nigga is mad as hell." Liyah

commented, as she laughed at the conversation I shared with Smooth. "Fuck him!" I spat. "He doesn't own me, and I'm not about to be his trophy anymore." I continued as I folded my arms. "Good for you girl." La'Tanya encouraged. "Yeah, that's my girl." Liyah said as she stroked the side of my face. "You know it." I smiled proudly. I loved the support I was getting from my new family. That was something I always lacked in life, and to finally have that was fulfilling. I looked over only to see 'Tanya's face go from joy to gloom. "You ok girl?" I asked with concern. "Yeah, I got a mild headache, I just need to go get some water, be right back." She replied as she quickly got up and headed into the house. I don't know what was going on with her, but the feeling at the pit of my stomach was telling me that I couldn't trust that bitch.

Introducing La'Tanya

After I excused myself, I made my way to the kitchen and fixed a glass of water to calm my nerves of the flashbacks popping in my head. I stood in front of the window watching the three little ones playing outside with Liyah. The plan was in session and eventually I would be getting back everything that was taken from me. I went through hell and back in my childhood, and when I finally got the life that I deserved, it was stolen like a thief in the night.

Flashback to 2004:

I moved from New York with my sister to Atlanta, in hopes of starting a new life. A life better than prostituting on the streets, living in a whore house, and struggling to survive. I never went to school, and I never had friends. My sister was my only friend, and hustling was the lesson I learned in the school of hard knocks. The life I lived in New York caused me to be a hard and emotionless bitch at the age of eighteen. Getting raped and beat by your pimp every night, after turning tricks all day; weekly trips to the clinic ending in either an abortion or with an STD, and crying yourself to sleep every night, can take a toll on you. I had to leave that hell hole and find a new way. Yet, money doesn't grow from trees, so in order for my sister Skipper and I to get on our feet while we were in Atlanta, we had to strip at Magic city, showing ass and titties for some bread.

Every night was the same routine, dress it up, strip it down, and get your money. Yet something about this night was different. "My cousin and his niggas are in the building bitches!" *My co-worker and acquaintance named Belle, announced as she entered the dressing room. A huge smile covered her brown face as her hazel eyes gleamed with excitement.* "Ooo, do they have money?" *Keisha,* aka "Bad-Ass" asked, as she was popping on her gum, and lacing up her corset. "Money? Girl these niggas is eating, drinking, and breathing money. They are the niggas from the Hot Boys Gang." Belle answered, causing all the girls to gasp in excitement. "The Hot Boys! Oh shit let me put my best lace front on tonight." Keisha exclaimed, as her and her little clique scrambled to get ready. I didn't know who, and where the Hot Boys came from, but all I knew was that they had money out the ass, and they were going to cash someone out tonight.

"'Tanya girl, I want you to work with me and Keisha up in V.I.P for my cousin and his boys' aiight?" Belle directed. "You want me?" I asked, as I looked around the room. I was still the newbie here, and only the baddest bitches who has been here for a long time, and earned a name for themselves could work in V.I.P. "Yeah girl, I said Tanya didn't I?" Belle said sarcastically as she sat at the booth next to me. "Hmm, she ain't on my level, you better tell her ass to sit the fuck back and let the bad bitches handle this." Keisha spat, as she stood there mugging me. "Shut the fuck up Keisha, everybody got to get their chance one day, just like you did." Belle snapped. "No!" Keisha popped her lips. "I worked for mine, that bitch never worked for shit. That's the difference between us". Keisha retorted, before exiting out of the dressing room. I laughed at the comment she just stated. She never worked for nothing in her life. Hell, if she walked in my shoes as a hustler, she wouldn't even last five minutes.

I never had any problems with any females at Magic City, but Keisha was the only one I truly disliked. She thought she was hot shit with her long, blonde lace front, light colored skin, and phat ass that would make Buffy the Body, and Bria Myles look twice. I'm not going to lie; Keisha had skills for days when it came to stripping. She could make the men cry at the strip club, but she was still an arrogant, nothing ass female. She had the privilege to grow up in the suburbs, attend a private school, and had the opportunity to get a full ride to college. Yet, after graduating high school with honors, this bitch would rather end up at the strip club! Like I said before, she was a nothing ass female. I hated seeing spoiled ass females who grew up with a silver spoon in their mouth, trying to be out here doing my hustle for fun. I didn't have a fucking choice nor the opportunity to go to school, and make something of myself. I was forced into this game and I don't think I'll ever see a way out... Until tonight that is!

"Girl, don't worry about that bitch, you know her ass is spoiled rotten." Belle said, breaking my thoughts. "Yeah, fuck her yo'." I said, as I applied my mascara in the mirror. "That bitch is mad dumb yo'! Bitches like that get killed back in my hood." I continued, in my thick New York accent. "I feel you girl." Belle laughed. "But c'mon, let's go make this money. My cousin just got in town and I want him to have a good time, and trust me, he has a thing for pretty Puerto Rican girls like you." She smiled. "Well shit, let's do it then!" I exclaimed, as I got up and followed Belle back into the club.

Anxiety crept up on me as I made my way up into the V.I.P room. Young Buck's "Shorty wanna ride with me" blasted as I spotted Keisha bent over, touching her toes, as her ass wildly vibrated and clapped for this sexy caramel man with braids. It was about twenty niggas in this room all smoking on weed and poppin' extremely expensive bottles of liquor. I felt like a fish out of water, as I scanned the room of men whose eyes were all on me.

"Come here mami." The deep voice greeted me from behind. I turned around only to see this sexy chocolate man with long braids, and grey eyes sitting *in the corner. I looked at Belle who was cheesing at me. "Go take care of my cousin girl." She yelled out, as she walked towards the group of thirsty niggas. One look at him, and I instantly became nervous. He was just so sexy.*

I quickly made my way over to his area, and began standing in front of him, dancing like I usually do. I was so nervous, but I continued shaking my ass for him. Out of nowhere, he grabbed me by my arm and pulled me down on top of him. "Come sit on this and show me what you are working with. Don't be shy." He whispered in my ear, as he grabbed my hips and guided me into a rhythm. As he requested, I began giving him the lap dance of his life. Nothing but hundreds was thrown in the air, and I loved it.

While still sitting on his lap, I bent over and grabbed my ankles as I bounced my ass wildly, one cheek at a time, then both cheeks. "Mmm, damn girl, you're a killa'." He groaned out in pleasure. I couldn't help but smile at his compliment, as I continued to show him my skills.

R. Kelly's "Slow Wind" began to play, as I slowed it down, and made it sexy for him. "Mmm, turn around girl; I want to take a good look at you from the front." My mysterious man commanded. I quickly turned around, still on his lap, and was now face to face with this sexy man. He stared at me with those sexy eyes and licked his luscious lips. "Damn, you are beautiful." He said astonished. I looked away and laughed shyly. "No, I'm serious." He said, as he gently caressed the side of my face. I looked back at him and saw the sincerity in his eyes. This was the first time a man looked at me and made me feel like a woman, not an object.

"What is your name?" He asked. "Tanya." I said lowly. "Why are you out here stripping Tanya?" He said with a serious face. No one ever called me by my real name, nor did anyone care enough to ask me why I was doing what I was doing. "I don't know." I responded softly. I didn't want him to know my story. After all, he was just a customer.

"You know why ma', but you just don't want to tell me. It's ok, I understand that you think I'm just a customer, but I can be more than that if you let me." He replied, slowing taking hold of my heart. "I want to know more about you. I want to get inside of your world and change it for you. Can I do that for you 'Tanya?" He suggested.

"I don't even know your name." I snapped. "My name is Kenny, but they call me K-dubb." He introduced. "Don't tell nobody my government name though. That's only between me and you." He laughed, showing off his pearly whites. I couldn't help but smile and blush in return. "So can I do that *for you?" He posed again, staring into my eyes. Damn, I couldn't resist him. Something about him brought chills up my spine. "Yes." I finally answered. "You made a good decision mami, go grab your stuff and let's go." K-dubb said as we both stood up. "Okay." I agreed and did what he said, no questions asked.*

With my bags in my hand, I made my way outside only to see K-dubb leaned against his all black Hummer 2, waiting patiently for me. I couldn't help but smile at this sight. "You ready baby?" K-dubb asked, as he grabbed my bags, and placed them in the back of his car. "Yes." I smiled righteously before hopping in his car. That night he drove me back to his hotel suite, and instead of trying to dick me down like the other guys I encountered in my life; he laid besides me, holding me tight and let me talk, telling him my story. I went from crying as I told him my life story, to laughing and being at ease. K-dubb made me feel something I never felt in my life, and I instantly fell in love with him that night.

Over time my relationship with K-dubb became stronger to the point of marriage. I was no longer the stripper at Magic City, I was now known as Mrs. Kenny Walker, the wife of a street legend. K-dubb and his crew were taking Atlanta by storm and I loved the benefits I received from it. Our twelve bedroom mansion was fabulous, and the eight cars we had were luxurious. I had a room for just storing my shoes, a room just for my expensive bags, and room for my clothes and accessories. Shit, we we're living the good life as my baby was out there making the bread. I didn't have to want, nor work for nothing! The money, power, and respect from just being the wifey of K-dubb was nice. Yet the love that we shared was even better. Late nights spent making love, and early mornings spent making that "after-sex" breakfast were amazing.

For all the good things K-dubb did in my life, I had no choice but to bare him a child as my appreciation. A year after marriage, and our daughter Kristina was born. She had the smooth brown skin, and grey eyes like her father and long wavy black hair like me. That was our baby, and our heart. Nothing could be better than this. I finally had what I've been missing my whole life. A family, a home, and love. I wouldn't trade anything in the world for what I've finally received, everything was perfect….until that day came.

The very next day after Kristina's 4th birthday party, I woke up only to see suitcases everywhere. K-dubb pranced back and forward throwing his clothes, shoes and jewelry in each suitcase. "Where are you going baby?" I asked still half asleep. "I got business to take care of baby. We got a meeting to attend to in the Dominican Republic." He explained as he sat on the bed next to me. "Oh, I got family over there babe, me and Kristina can come and visit while you handle business." I suggested as I sat up with excitement. "No!" He interjected. "What?" I replied in confusion. Any other time K-dubb would always let me go with him on his business trips, so why the sudden change this time?

"It'll be too dangerous, and I want you and our baby to be safe ok?" He continued sweetly. I sighed in response. I love my man and I didn't want to upset him by starting an argument. "Ok baby." I replied submissively. "That's my girl!" K-dubb smiled and kissed me on the cheek. "How about you help me pack up, I got to be out of here by ten." He suggested. With no questions asked, I helped him pack up his suitcases and placed them in his car.

"You are so good to me Tanya." K-dubb said as

he caressed my face. Tears cascaded down my face as I held Kristina up on my hip, and was embraced by my husband. "I don't want you to leave baby." I said softly. "I know ma', I don't want to leave you guys either. But business has to be made, and I'll be back… I promise." He reassured. "I know you will." I smiled. "Aiight, well let me go and make this money, I'll call you every day I promise." He said as he hopped into his truck. After sharing our last kiss and exchanging our goodbyes, I watched as K-dubb drove off. I wanted to believe everything was going to be fine, but something in the pit of my stomach was telling me otherwise.

Two months later

I woke up in the bed with Kristina lying next to me looking like an angel. She looked so peaceful just the way her father did when he was sleep. I still couldn't wrap my head around the fact the he just up and left us. I slid out of the bed, and made my way through the cold lonely house, that was once filled with warmth and love. I walk into the kitchen, grabbed the house phone, and immediately dialed Kenny's number. My heart dropped as the phone as the operator said the line has been disconnected, still the same old song. Why do I keep doing this to myself?

He has been gone for two months now on this business trip, and he hasn't even called to check on us since he first landed. That's when I knew something wasn't right, and I began to have a feeling that he was never coming back. I was stuck in my own thoughts when a loud knock interrupted my thoughts. I rush to the front door thinking it was Kenny, but when I open the door, there stood a white man in a nice black tailor-made suit.

"Yes, what do you want?" I asked nonchalantly,

while slightly opening the door. "May I speak to the owner of the house please?" the White man asked. "I am the owner…" I replied with an attitude. "Well Mrs. Walker the payments on the house and your eight vehicles has not been paid in over eight months. So we are here to collect the collateral. We tried to inform your co-signer whose name is on the contract… A Mr. Williams, but the number he has listed was disconnected." The man explained, leaving me in confusion.

"A Mr. Who? I think you have the wrong people here sir, my husband Kenny Walker is the co-signer of this house and as well as the cars! So I 'am positive that it has been paid in full." I said to clarify this mishap. "No ma'am, I'm pretty sure that this is the right address. You have the two primary cars that are a black Hummer 2 and a black range rover? And then the other six cars are…." The man continued to list out all the cars that we owned. "I want to talk to your supervisors!" I interjected with rage.

"Ma'am I don't think you understand we are here to collect what is ours. You have thirty minutes to collect your clothes and exit the property." The man said sternly. I stood there in shock, as he served me the paperwork. A flatbed truck pulled up to repossess my cars, and a moving truck came to take everything in the house away from me. I stood there with tears in my eyes, as I looked over the paperwork and immediately spotted the signature of a Kentrell Williams! I couldn't believe my eyes… This mothafucka' had the crack head from downtown sign the contract for our home and cars!

I ran upstairs to pack whatever I could in my suitcases, and called for a cab to pick us up. As we rode off in the cab, my daughter asked me a million and one questions, all of which I didn't even have the answer for. I told her to hush as I called the private investigator I recently hired to find Kenny. My mouth *flew open when he told me that a "Kenny Walker" didn't not exist, and that this mysterious man didn't leave a trail behind. Everything that I thought was in our name was in another man's name, and on top of that, all my bank accounts were frozen. I couldn't believe this the man I was married to for four years was a fake, an imposter. I had a child by this man, and didn't even know who he was! Don't even know his real name. I had a stranger in my bed for four fuckin' years! Now here I am with nowhere to go, and with no money, just had four hundred dollars left to my name? How am I going to explain to my daughter that her daddy isn't coming back? I promise when I find him, wherever he is, he is going to pay for humiliating me like this. Leaving me here with nothing, not even a pot to piss in!*

My daughter and I lived on the streets, or jumped from shelter to shelter for months. Finally when my sister Skipper and her husband Remeko came back from the Virgin Islands, she let us live with her. Although I barely heard from her while we were both married to our husbands, I was grateful for my loving sister to let me in, once again she was truly all I had.

To help me cope with the depression I was going through, Remeko provided me some of his finest, imported potent drugs, aka that 'White girl' to help calm my nerves each day. Everything was finally getting under control until one night of too much 'White girl'. I laid out in my bed staring at the ceiling fan in fascination. With the combination of drugs and it being the hottest day in Atlanta, I had no choice but to lay in my bed naked. Everyone in the house was gone, so there shouldn't be a problem to be butt naked in my own bedroom. Or so I thought.

"Yo 'Tanya, you want some more white---" Remeko paused as he barged into my bedroom. I was so drugged up; I couldn't even jump up and cover my body in response. All I could do was look at him and whisper "No, I'm good." "Mmm, you sure you're good?" Remeko said, as he walked over to me. His eyes roamed my thick body as I just stared at him. I would be lying to say that Remeko wasn't fine as hell. Standing at 6'5", with smooth chocolate brown skin, long black dreadlocks that fell down to his mid-back, and the ripped body to die for; it was hard not to be turned on by him.

"It's hot in here isn't it?" He asked in his sexy Jamaican accent. "Yes." I replied softly. "Let me take these off and cool us down." He suggested, as he took off his wife beater and walked out of the bedroom. Within two minutes, Remeko came back into the bed room with a bucket of ice. "Now let me cool you off baby." He said, as he hovered over me and reached for some ice.

I laid there as Remeko placed the cube of ice over my nipples, causing me to shiver. "Mmm" I moaned out from the pleasure I received from the ice and his tongue over my nipple. It was so wrong but it felt so right. I haven't had pleasure in so long, and what my sister doesn't know won't hurt her right?

I closed my eyes and gripped the sheets as Remeko was eating my pussy out with the help of the ice. "Damn this is so good baby." I squealed as I came on his tongue. "Mmmm, wait 'til you feel this dick." Remeko said as he came up for air, and began to kiss me. I held him closely as we continued to kiss passionately. I gasped for air as I felt his thick eleven inches enter my wet warmth below, and embraced his torso with my legs as he pumped in and out of me slowly. I couldn't help but moan loudly from the pleasure my sister's husband was giving me. I was so into it that when I opened my eyes, I was greeted by my sister standing in the doorway, staring at us in shock. Instead of jumping up, and stopping him, all I could do was say "Mmm, keep going baby...Don't stop."

To my surprise my sister calmly walked away and closed the door behind her. Skipper was never the one to be rowdy, and start mess so I figured she wouldn't trip. Yet when it was time to have family dinner, Remeko suddenly croaked over after eating his curry chicken and rice, and I was being charged by my sister with a butcher's knife in her hand. The kids and I hid in attic until the police came. That crazy bitch deserved to get arrested. Unfortunately, I was now left to take care of not only my daughter but my niece.

I was now back to square one, living in a shelter, now with two kids to provide for. There was no other way to survive; I had to go back to stripping and tricking to make some money to provide for my family and I. "Well welcome back bitch! I knew you weren't going to live that fabulous life for long." Keisha, aka Bad Ass snarled as I walked into the dressing room of Magic City. The other strippers laughed and made rude comments as I made my way to my old booth. None of the females that I was once cool with stripped here anymore; it was either the new booties or the old heads that were taking over the game. I felt like a fish out of water in this strip club.

Minding my own business, I began to put my outfit and make-up on. "I just came to say hello girls." A sultry and familiar voice protruded from the background. I turned around only to spot Belle, my old female acquaintance and the cousin of K-dubb.

Belle didn't even look like the old stripper I use to know. Her smooth brown skin glowed under the fluorescent light, as her long, blue-black, Brazilian weave was styled in gorgeous Kim Kardashian curls, and her Smokey eye was done to perfection, complimenting her natural hazel eyes. She rocked nothing but blinged out Tiffany jewelry around her neck, ring and arm, and her slim but curvy body was poured into a sexy peach dress, and Balenciaga gladiator heels to match. I don't know what she did, and how she did it, but baby girl was rollin' in dough.

"Oh my gosh! 'Tanya is that you?" She exclaimed, as she ran over and hugged me. "Girl I haven't seen you since the wedding, how you been? And what are you doing here?" She continued, as she looked at me in confusion. I looked back at her, shocked that she didn't know what happened between her cousin and I. "You didn't know?" I asked. "Know what?" She replied. "Girl her man left her ass! High and dry. Left her with no money, and not even a pot to piss in. Her and her daughter has been on the streets." Keisha gladly interjected, telling the whole world my business…as if they didn't know already. Belle looked at me with shock written all over her face.

"How could he have done that to you?" She said, as she sat down in the chair next to me. I couldn't even hold it in; I sat down in my chair and cried, something I haven't really done in a while. "I can't believe him, that's some fucked up shit Kris pulled right there." Belle commented as she held me in her arms. "Kris? I'm talking about Kenny." I said, as I quickly jumped out her arms. "Umm, Kenny? I don't know a Kenny but his name is Kris… aka K-dubb." Belle said, looking at me like I had two heads.

"He told me his name was Kenny." I said, as my blood boiled. "Well girl he lied to you. Kris is up in Detroit now, making moves with the Hot Boyz." Belle explained. "In Detroit?" I posed. "Yep, he been up there for almost a year now, ain't that right Liyah?"

Belle turned to ask some girl standing by the door. "This is Liyah. She is one of the members of the Hot Boyz. Shit, the only female in the whole damn thing!" Belle exclaimed.

I looked over to see a caramel girl with long braids, dressed in all black posted by the door. She looked familiar, I might've seen her a couple of times with K-dubb, but never really talked to her. "Yep, he sho' has been up in tha' D with the rest of us." Liyah replied. "So he has been up there this whole time?" I asked in disbelief.

"Yep. He been up there girl, I thought you knew. I know I been over in New York and Miami since I last seen you, so I thought things were good in your hood. I came over to your mansion and seen that it was seized. I tried to call you…" Belle started. "But it was cut off." I finished. "Yeah, so I got worried. I'm only in town for this week so I decided to stop by my old workplace and see the girls, and now I'm running into you. This is a mess. I can't believe K-dubb would do you like this. He needs to get his ass beat for real." Belle continued, as I sat there in a daze.

"Damn he did you dirty, I knew this was going to happen but I couldn't say anything. It's kind of a Hot Boyz honor to keep shit to yourself. All them niggas had a pact about what happens in Atlanta, stays in Atlanta. But to string you along for five years, knowing he got a girl back at home in Detroit, that's grimey fa' sho my baby." Liyah added into the conversation. To hear that K-dubb had a girl back at home caused my blood to boil even more. "That son of a bitch!" I yelled, as I stood up and pushed everything off the makeup counter. I couldn't hold it in anymore, I had to let it out. I tore that dressing room up, throwing chairs and punching mirrors. I snapped! Liyah and Belle had to calm me down, before I did anything crazier.

"I'm going to kill that nigga!" I repeated over and over again. "I'm going to kill him…" "I'm not mad at you for doing it girl." Belle said, as she rocked me back and forward in her arms. "Shit, I can help you if you want." Liyah said, as she stood there and sparked a blunt. "Oh yeah?" I looked at her full of excitement at the thought. "Hell yeah." She replied, as she exhaled her smoke. "I don't even like that snake. I can give you all the info you need, and show you how and when to get that ass." Liyah finished.

"Well let's do it then." I said, smiling at the thought. It was time for me to take what was taken from me, my life. Belle laughed at our conversation. "Ya'll are crazy, I know you're mad right now, but once you calm down you will be aiight girl." She began. "I'm going to head back out there with the girls. Holla' if you need me." Belle chimed in as she stood up, and walked out the exit, leaving Liyah and I alone.

"I don't know what you on, but I was serious about taking that mothafucka' out." Liyah said, as she sat in the chair looking at me. "And I was serious too." I replied, staring into her eyes. "I like you." Liyah smiled. "You seem like a real bitch 'Tanya, and I only fuck with the real, not the fake." She continued. "Well K-dubb wasn't real at all." I commented. "And that's exactly why I don't fuck with that nigga. All he is to me and to the Hot Boyz gang is a worker." Liyah chuckled. Just then, a group of strippers walked into the room, breaking our attention.

"It's too hot to talk about what's about to go down up in this bitch…" Liyah started, as her eyes followed the phat ass of one of the strippers walking past. "How about you come to my hotel suite and we can talk about it." She suggested, and with no hesitation I said, "I'm down."

After the first night spent at Liyah's suite, we spent weeks and weeks plotting on our revenge against K-dubb. During that time Liyah and I became close. She was known as "Big Daddy" out on the streets and I could see why. Liyah provided anything I wanted and more, including a house and a car for my family and I. Although trust was a hard thing to come by, I grew to trust Liyah overtime.

Words couldn't explain how much I appreciated all she has done for me. Especially at the moment that K-dubb laid on the cement with those grey eyes that use to send chills down my spine now looking up at me pleading for his life. A smile crept over my face as I cocked my gun and pulled the trigger, sending him to his maker. As the blood spilled out his body, it felt as if all the anger and sadness that I felt over the years finally came to an end. It was all thanks to Liyah. There was nothing in the world I wouldn't do to repay her.

After the death of K-dubb I felt like I can finally live my life with no regrets yet there was still something missing, even though I got my revenge for what he did to me I still wasn't satisfied. At the end of the day he was my husband and the thought that all these chicks were playing my role made me sick! I could never truly accept these bitches as my comrades but for the sake of my niece and my child I would play my role and continue to provide them with the best.

<u>Simone</u>

Today was the day of the verdict. While many people were busy heading home for the holidays, I was sitting here waiting on my final verdict. As I sat in the courthouse next to Pistol, waiting for the judge to come, my hands trembled. Never in my life have I been so nervous than I was today. "Calm down Simone," Pistol placed his hand over my trembling fist. "I got you, don't worry about it." He winked at me before we stood up as the judge made her entrance. She was a short, chubby, Cuban woman with a stern face. She was known as Judge Gladiator out on the streets, since she was known to slaughter niggas when it came to their sentencing. So far this was not looking too good for me.

I sat back and watched this trial unfold; pictures of Jake's murder were being displayed for the jury to see, as well as pictures of his brother Jayden's house that was burned to ashes. The sight boiled my blood even more, I knew I was guilty as charged, but I had faith in Pistol to pull me out of this one. "Your honor, there is no way that my client could have possibly killed two men at the same time. New found evidence has shown that Mr. Jayden Shamir's death was caused by a normal house fire that was caused by an oven mitt being placed on the stove. Before that, Mr. Shamir was prescribed a high dosage of sleeping pills that were proven to be something he utilized for his drug addiction. Could it have been possible that he overdosed on these pills and fell asleep, unaware of the accidental oven mitt being placed on the stove?" Pistol argued.

"Hmm," The judge nodded her head in response. "Did the D.A ever find evidence of what really killed Mr. Shamir?" She asked. "No ma'am, they could never pin point anything because they automatically pinned it on my client as arson and murder." Pistol spat. "Objection!" The other lawyer yelled out in anger. "Overruled" The judge replied. "Continue on sir." She directed back to Pistol.

"Your honor, they had no evidence of my client being anywhere near the scene of both crimes that day. Yet somehow the crimes have been placed on her. Why? That is the question. Since the two Shamir brothers, Jake and Jayden were both the leaders of a huge gang affiliation, there are tons of other possible suspects that could have been linked to the murder. Even those such as Officer Lorenzo, the same officer who arrested my client for the murder of the two men. We found out that he planted evidence to frame her for the murder he committed." Pistol explained.

"And how do you know this?" The judged asked with a raised eyebrow. "We have a confession tape your honor." Pistol answered, causing everyone in the courtroom to gasp in shock. Shit, he even had me in shock, how did he ever pull this off? I sat back and watched the as the video revealed the Mexican man crying during his confession. The man gave every minor detail of how and why he killed the two. He was so good at it, that he even had me believing that he killed them! Although, Pistol and I both knew that I was the only one who killed those two traitors. Yet the video sold them all, by the time we finally reached the verdict I was acquitted of all charges, and free to go out into the real world. Free to go out and seek my revenge.

The sun shined down on me as I was finally released out of prison. I couldn't help but smile as I walked up to Pistol, who was standing outside the gate, leaning on his black Bentley coupe. I hugged him tightly as I thanked him over and over again. "No problem, it was only right that I take care of someone who is family to me." He said, as he broke the hug and looked into my eyes that were filled of tears of appreciation. "You're right, we are like family." I replied. "Closer than blood." He nodded. "Yeah, closer than blood." I agreed. Pistol was right, back when we're in the Hot Boyz gang Pistol and I use to make hits together whenever Kris punked out, or had "other plans." The only person in the gang that I could really trust to have my back was Pistol. He was loyal to me, and I was loyal to him. Even though life separated us, we still had a close bond.

"Well c'mon ma', we got to hurry up and go catch this plane to NYC since we got things to do and people to see." Pistol said, as he walked over to his side of the car. Without another word said, I quickly hopped into his car, ready for whatever that was about to go down. "There is a lot of shit going on that I need to update you on." Pistol began, as he zoomed down the freeway. "I'm all ears." I replied, as I sat back and enjoyed the wind blowing through my hair. "There has been a big separation between Liyah and Smooth, especially since Liyah took Sweetz away from him." "Liyah took Sweetz?" I asked in confusion. "Yeah, I'm guessing you didn't know that Liyah and Sweetz are lovers, and has been since Sweetz stopped fucking with Kris." Pistol answered, leaving me in pure shock. "Sweetz was fuckin' Kris!" I said full of mixed emotions. Not only was Kris fucking with La'Tanya, but he was fuckin' with Sweetz? My only friend, the only female I kept close to me, and she had the nerve to sleep with my man behind my back!

"Yeah, Sweetz and Kris been fuckin' since shit, back in '03 I think." Pistol scratched his head. "Yeah I think so, all I know was that Sweetz was fifteen when she was fuckin' him, even got pregnant by him... but he made her go the clinic." Pistol further explained as my blood boiled. All this shit that was kept secret from me, and that whole time they were all in my face smiling like everything was all good. The nerves of those fake bitches. "Sweetz was supposed to be my friend." I said as I looked out the window. "Yeah, well ain't too many friends up in the Hot Boyz world. Shit the only reason we got close was because of our hits. If it wasn't for that, I wouldn't even talk to you at all. I don't fuck with member's girlfriends... too risky." Pistol said, speaking real shit. "I feel you though, it is risky. But how did you know about Sweetz and Kris?" I interrogated.

Pistol

I smiled as Simone asked me about Sweetz and Kris. There was so much shit to this sick web of the Hot Boyz that she didn't even have a clue. I kind of felt bad for telling her all of the secrets that were kept hidden from her, but shit the truth had to come out one day. I sighed as the memories of my haunted past came flooding back. "I found out about Sweetz and Kris because he took her to the mansion late one night while Smooth was out of town doing business…"

Flashback:

Sweetz came into the mansion, stumbling and being loud because she was so drunk. That was the only reason why I woke up off the couch, since I passed out from my midnight "smoke session." My eyes opened and landed on Sweetz dressed in a sexy red teddy and heels to match. "Sweetz what the fuck are you doing here dressed like that?" I yelled, as I stood up and walked over to her. "Man leave her alone." Kris jumped in. "And what the fuck are you doing with her Kris?" I turned towards him, getting into his face. "This is my baby girl, I can do what I want nigga." Kris replied, getting bold with me. Smooth was my brother and I wasn't about to let this nigga disrespect him like that, in our home at that. "What the fuck are you doing with Smooth's girl?" I snapped. "Doing what he needs to be doing, fucking her!" Kris exclaimed. "Is this true Sweetz?" I asked as I turned towards her. "Yes...." She answered softly.

"Smooth never gives me attention, or treats me how I want to be treated or pleases me the way I need to. I just need my body taken care of every now and then." She continued, looking at me with those sad baby doll eyes. I sighed as I finally gave up. "Aiight you guys do what you do. I'm staying out of it." I said, throwing up my hands and walking away. "No..." She pleaded, as she grabbed my arm and pulled me closer to her. "Why don't you stay in it, why don't you join us?" She said softly as she looked at me seductively.

I always thought Sweetz was a pretty girl that any man would love to have. That pretty brown skin, pretty smile, and that sexy slim and curvy body... A man would be a fool not to want her. I wanted to say no, but as I stood there debating, she began to strip out her clothes right then and there. Damn, I couldn't resist.

I grabbed her little ass and carried her into the guest room down the hall. I laid her down on the bed as I began kissing on her from head to toe. I got so caught up in the lust, that I forgot the fact that she was Smooth's girl. She laid there and moaned as Kris and I began sucking and licking on her nipples. It was double the pleasure for her and she loved it. The Hot Boyz always had a rep for running trains on women, so sharing her with Kris was not a problem. I pounded that sweet little pussy as she sucked Kris off, and she loved it. The things Sweetz did to us was unbelievable. The porn stars didn't have shit on

Sweetz. The sweet and innocent girl, who I once knew, was now a nasty and certified freak that brought me to maximum pleasure. It was bittersweet, fucking not only the girlfriend of my gang's leader, but the girlfriend of my own brother. And now that I was fucking her along with Kris, I had to keep this a secret in order to cover my ass.

"After that night, I never touched her since. One time was enough for me, and I regret it." I sighed. "Wow." Was all Simone could say in response. "Yeah, I know." I added. "Damn I'm really speechless. That was some sick shit." She said astonished. "Running trains and shit..." Her voice trailed off. "If you think that shit is sick, wait 'til I tell you about Liyah." I replied.

Flashback:

When Smooth formed the Hot Boyz, he had no intentions of letting his little sister and brother in the gang. Yet, with the lack of manpower, he needed to take in all the people he could in order to become the next powerful gang in the streets. Smooth recruited over sixty new members in a matter of one month, but trust still had to be earned.

"Please let me join." Smooth's younger brother Mike would ask after our meetings. "Hell no, I'm not about let you in this lifestyle." Smooth answered. "No blood of mine will be out here on these streets…. Not while I'm still living." Smooth was determined, but things had changed. Our sixty members dwindled down to only ten, due to the police enforcement taking over, and our rival gangs killing them off. With only ten men on his side, he had to bring in whoever he could to help start the Hot Boyz from the ground up… It was time for initiation.

Halloween was supposed to be a night of fun, but since it was the night of initiation for the Hot Boyz

Gang, it was also known as the night of terror for those in Detroit area. Most of us robbed or killed random niggas, raped women, or took out a whole community in a drive-by. Sounds tragic, but shit, it is what is it. Everyone had successfully made it through initiation, even Smooth's little brother Mike; but the only person who wasn't crossed over, was Liyah.

We all came back to the house excited for our new membership for a lifetime with the Hot Boyz. We celebrated, drinking our night away, while Smooth sat in his chair staring off into space. "You aiight man?" I asked, as I placed my hand on his shoulder. "Yeah, I will be…" He replied seriously, as he stood up. "Aiight ya'll! It's time to initiate one more person." He announced loudly. "Pistol, grab that box of condoms and ya'll follow me upstairs." He commanded. I grabbed the big box of magnums as I was told, and followed Smooth upstairs.

We made our way to Liyah's room, only to see her lying there in her pink pajamas sleeping peacefully in her bed. I didn't even have the heart to try and witness what was about to go down. She was only fifteen, and the only way she was going to be introduced to the gang was by getting sexed in. I instantly got sick to my stomach at the thought.

"Liyah wake up." Smooth said as he pulled the covers from her. "What's going on?" She mumbled, as she wiped her eyes. She looked just like an angel, with that sweet and innocent face, light brown eyes and long curly hair that flowed down her back. She was too sweet to be in this lifestyle, and sad thing was that she didn't even have a clue on what was about to go down. "Take off your clothes." Smooth commanded sternly. "My what?" She jumped up in the bed as she looked at all eleven of us in the room.

"You heard me Liyah, do it now!" He yelled as

his eyes turned cold black. "Porque?" She cried out in Spanish. "It's time for you to join the gang." Smooth answered before he chugged down the rest of his bottle of E&J. "But I don't wanna..."She cried harder. "Fuck what you want. Just do it Liyah... Or I'll kill you!" Smooth yelled, as he pulled out his gun and pointed at her.

Scared of the threat, Liyah took off her clothes and laid there as each one of us took our turn taking her virginity. She laid there and cried, and cried, and cried. Yet nothing could be worse than what was going to come next. "The only way to finish this off is through me." Smooth said coldly. We all looked at him in disgust. Was this nigga really about to have sex with his own little sister? "Noooo... Smooth No!" She yelled, as he crawled into the bed. By this time she was too weak to move out of the bed. Having eleven niggas in and out of her was enough. "Shut the fuck up!" He slapped her. "Now close your fuckin' *eyes and it will be over in a minute." He continued as he held her down and began to finish the "initiation."*

"After that, Liyah was never the same again. The sweet and innocent Liyah was gone. She hated Smooth for what happened to her. Shit, that was the reason why she turned into a lesbian. That night fucked her up." I further explained.

"Damn..." Simone said as she shook her head. "The fucked up shit we all had to go through for the love of the Hot Boyz." She continued. "You got that shit right. Everyone has their own motives, and when you put them together it will all cause each one of us to destruct in any shape, way, or form." I said, before we hopped out the rental coupe and made our way into the airport. After sleeping through most of the flight, we safely made it back to the good ole New York. I knew Simone had a lot on her mind since we drove in silence as I drove us to my condo in

Manhattan.

<u>Simone</u>

I thought about what Pistol said as we continued to make our way to his place. All of our motives were causing us to destruct in some way or another. Everyone linked to the Hot Boyz were dropping like flies. The "family" we once were was truly coming to end, especially since I'm back home.

Finally arriving to Pistol's condo, I stepped in happy to be out the cold. Yet only to be greeted by someone who looked like a brown skin beauty queen, dressed in an all-white sweater dress and leggings on this cold winter day. "Welcome back into the world!" She giggled as she hugged me. "Umm..." I looked at Pistol like who the fuck is this? "This is my wife Belle." He introduced. "Nice to finally meet you. D'wayne told me all about you." Belle gleamed, as she broke the hug and smiled in my face. "Oh D'wayne huh? Well nice to finally meet his wife." I replied uneasy. I haven't met a female so happy like that since I met Sweetz; and with trust being a hard thing to come by, it was kind of hard to be all nicey-nicey to this broad.

"Baby the mechanic called and said he will be over later on tonight to come look at the Benz." Belle started. "Aiight. Let me go change out these clothes and we will go to our Christmas party." Pistol replied, before giving her a peck on the lips. "Ok baby." She gleamed, as she watched him walk back towards the master bedroom. "So you're the infamous Krazy that I've been hearing about huh?" Belle began, switching the conversation over to me. "Depending on what you heard yeah that's me." I said harshly, as I looked her up and down. "Oh no girl, I'm not trying to come at you foully, actually I knew about you through Kris." She finished. "Kris?" I frowned up my face in confusion. "What you know about Kris?" I asked. "I'm his cousin...well was his cousin..." Belle started to tear up as she answered. "Didn't know Kris had family," was all I could say in response.

"Yeah, we were first cousins since our dads were brothers. I used to live in the ATL, so whenever he was down there we would link up. Shit I even introduced him to 'Tanya...Oops!" She paused, realizing that she had said too much. "It's aiight, I already knew about that shit." I said to put her at ease. "I'm really sorry for the fucked up shit he did... No female deserves the treatment that Kris put you and the others through." Belle sympathized as she stared into my eyes. I nodded in acceptance.

"Yeah, what he did was fucked up. Shit what we all did was fucked up. It is what is it is when you are a part of this street life." I replied bluntly. I couldn't help being so cold to people, when you lived the lifestyle that I lived you have no other choice than to be a cold hearted bitch. "I understand" Belle said sincerely. Yet I knew this bitch didn't have a clue of the ins and outs of the Hot Boyz. To be honest, she should be thanking God that she wasn't a part of this mess.

"I'm ready to go babe." Pistol interjected, quickly interrupting our conversation. "Ok well nice meeting you." Belle said, as she gathered her belongings. "Same here" I faked a smile, knowing that I really didn't give a damn. I had no desire in making new female friends. I only had a burning desire to kill off all the bitches who fucked me over.

As soon as Pistol and Belle left, I hopped in the shower to get myself ready for the day when the doorbell rung, I stuck my head out the shower to make sure that I wasn't trippin' but sure enough it was the doorbell. I hopped out the shower, slipped on my robe, and wrapped my hair in a towel as I made my way to the door. I quickly opened the door to a surprise. I couldn't even believe what I was seeing.

Tears filled my eyes as I was greeted by those almond shaped chocolate brown eyes. My lips tried to form his name but it just sat there on the tip of my tongue. I gazed up at his 6'4 frame which was in an auto mechanic jumpsuit with oil stains but that didn't even bother me because his body was just so thick and muscular, with those dreads that I use to pull when we made passionate sex was now hanging past his shoulder blades. "How you been young thang?" His deep voice filled my ears.

"Gutta!" I squealed his name in excitement "Yeah it's me." He smiled. Last time I seen him was the night he got locked up and was sentenced for 15 to 20 years. Now he is standing right before me.

"How and when did you get out?" I asked in disbelief. "Does it even matter? I missed you so much." He answered, while grabbing me into his arms. As he embraced me all of the old emotions came rushing back. The same emotions I buried when Kris came back into my life.

"You just don't know how fucked up I've been since you left. I feel so stupid, if I just would have listened to you, I wouldn't be going through this shit right now." I shared, while tears flowed down my face. "I'mma fix it ok?" Gutta consoled me, gently wiping the tears from my eyes. "How Gutta? You just don't know how deep this shit is…" I started but was abruptly cut off by Gutta. "It doesn't even matter how we do it, just know we can fix it. But right now I just want to enjoy you…Is that possible?" He said with a sneaky grin before he shut the door behind him. Without any hesitation, I dropped my robe and allowed Gutta to fully enjoy me. Seeing and getting some much need loving from Gutta was the best Christmas present a girl could ask for after being in lockdown for 4 years!

Over the next four months, Gutta and I became stronger than ever. He was now my right hand man, helping me plan a surefire way to seek my revenge. It felt good to get back to my old ways of making hits, yet this time was for a better reason; to get my son back. Anticipation seeped through my body as we sat in an all-black car that blended into the dark alley where we were currently parked. It was time to hold a stake out on our first victim.

<u>Smooth</u>

"Alright guys it's getting late and I know you want to go home so I'll do you a favor and say our meeting is adjourned, and we will come back in the morning to brainstorm on what's next." I announced, as I stared at the many faces that filled up my board room.

It was eleven o'clock on a Friday night and I knew that these people were tired of being stuck in this room talking about business. If this was back in my days of running the streets these niggas wouldn't be getting no sleep. If there was money to be made, then it would be getting handled at all hours of the night. Sleep is for the mothafuckas who are too comfortable in their broke ass lifestyle. Workers work and I get paid. Yet, the business world is a little different and for the first time of my life, I had to actually abide by the law, something that I've never been too keen of.

"Are you sure you want me to leave? Is there anything else that I could do for you sir?" The voice of my sexy Latina assistant graced my ears after everyone else scurried home. Her hands roamed from shoulders down my eight pack and finally connected to my dick. Any other time I would take this lovely lady up on her offer of giving me head until I could no longer bust, yet tonight wasn't one of those nights.

"Naw, we're good tonight Melina" I answered, as I removed her hands off me and got out of my leather chair. "Aww papi... why not tonight?" She pouted, as her cute accent came on full throttle. "Got a lot of shit on my mind that I need to sort out and take care of." I replied sternly. She sighed in response. "Ok papi, but promise me I can have a taste of it tomorrow morning?" I couldn't help but laugh. "Sure Melina." "Ok, goodnight sexy" She giggled, before grabbing her belongings and walking out my office. Finally, I had solitude.

I sat back at my desk and began to think about what was next. Shit has been out of hand since Sweetz left. Liyah has been controlling all the broads that were associated with the Hot Boyz. The only reason for this was to get back at me for all the foul shit that I've done to Liyah. But if taking Sweetz and my son up under her control was what one would call karma for all the fucked up shit that I did, then that truly wasn't shit. I know I have a tendency of controlling and ruining the lives of others around me, but I can't help it, it's how the game made me. Shit, it's in my genes, my father Big Man ran the streets of Detroit and some parts of New York, so stepping over a few wouldn't make him lose sleep at night, and neither will I.

When our father died, someone had to take his place and also take care of our family. Liyah should be thankful that I provided for her. So many thoughts flooded through my head as I stared out the window facing the city that never sleeps. Just the view inspired me to do more, maybe help the Hot Boyz down in Atlanta to prevent their demise. It makes me proud to know that I am the creator of all this and even the one who purposely destroyed the Hot Boyz in Detroit.

I knew all along what Kris and Krazy did to my father. I knew that Kris was a bitch that couldn't handle his own hits and had his main chick do all the dirty work for him. How could he possibly be a leader of any gang if he couldn't handle his own shit and take on a little bloodshed?

I also wasn't dumb to the fact that Kris was fucking Sweetz on the low. I knew it was going to happen when I saw the lust in his eyes when he first met her. He was never the loyal type. Not loyal to his woman, not loyal to his family, and not even loyal to his own damn self! Kris was nothing but a walking, talking contradiction. Which is why I planned his death. I set Kris up when he least expected it, and strategically planned for Krazy and Sweetz to meet the men they claimed they "loved" when they moved to LA. Although they were my half-brothers, to me those niggas were not my blood. I knew Krazy would snap and kill them off, which would do me a favor and get rid of them. This game was only made for one leader to be in power, and that would only be me.

To place my three opponents six feet under, I used Krazy and Sweetz as my pawns. Krazy getting locked up to take the fall for the deaths of Jake and Jayden was the next step of my plan. As for Sweetz, I knew it was a matter of time before that confused hoe would go crazy on her own. I didn't have to do much. Her role was to only have my son who would eventually take on my throne over the Hot Boyz gang in ATL. I left Mi'quel something to keep him informed just in case something were to happen to me. But I doubt it, because I am the mastermind behind it all. I plotted this whole thing from years on out, and I loved how it all panned out. Revenge is sweet, but knowing you created it is even better.

"Don't fuckin' move," the deep voice traveled from behind me, as I felt the barrel of a gun connect to the back of my head.

I sat there trying to figure out who in their right mind would dare put a gun to my fucking head! Rage filled within me, as I sat there powerless to a mothafucka who clearly had no clue who they were dealing with. The deep voice instructed who I assume their partner to tie me up. When I heard the sound of heels clicking across my wooden floors in my office, it finally hit me.

"So you finally came for me huh Krazy?" I said with a smirk on my face. I felt her sharp nails graze the back of my neck as she walked into my view. She was dressed to impress in her black leather pants, red leather thigh-high boots, and a red leather biker jacket to match. Her hair flowed past her shoulder blades with bright red streaks. I had to admit the little bitch was sexy.

Krazy smirked as she shackled me down to my office chair with chains. She slid onto my desk and crossed her legs, before she stared dead into my eyes. Those green eyes that seemed to be so cold, yet dead at the same time. I knew what this bitch was trying to do and it wasn't going to work! I was the boss of all bosses! No nigga and no bitch was going to have me shook! She pulled her blade out of her boot and began to clean her nails as she started to talk slow and calmly.

"This a nice office you got here Smooth...all nicely furnished and shit, you must just have money to blow huh?" She giggled. "But I'm a little surprised at how out in the open you've been living lately. Seems to me you got a little too comfortable with your routine...Like no one can reach out and touch you." She continued.

"Well Krazy, who in their right mind would touch me? Why would they touch someone with so much power and pull like I got?" I laughed. "Oh power and pull aye?" She responded, before she slid off the desk and slammed the knife into my hand. I heard the bones cracking and felt my veins slicing in half as she put pressure down onto the knife. As she twisted it slowly, it took every ounce of me not to scream. I bit down on my lip while staring straight into her eyes. I will be damned if I let this little bitch hear or see me in pain. I glared at her with every ounce of hate in my body.

"You know what Smooth, you disgust me...You are the most stupid, sick and twisted nigga I ever known. So you tellin' me that all you wanted and ever cared about was power? You really can sit here proud? Knowing you betrayed, hurt, and killed yo' family, friends, and other loved ones just for the sake of power and revenge! Well let me inform you on a little somethin', you fucked up when you betrayed me, and when you crossed him." She said, while pointing in a specific direction.

I felt the pressure of the gun leave the back of my head as deep voice revealed his identity. I blinked my eyes because I swore on everything I love they was playing tricks on me as I seen Gutta standing in front of me. Mann I didn't know Krazy was going to come back this hard. I remember when I played this nigga way back in the day. Just to feel this nigga's presence made my body shiver. I should've killed that nigga when I had the chance, and now this is the price I have to pay for making that little mistake. Just looking at him and down the barrel of his gun I knew there was no way in hell I was leaving this office without a bullet to my skull. So, I relaxed my body and prepared myself to go out like the boss that I am. I stared Gutta down as his finger pulled the trigger.

Introducing Gutta

I blew that nigga's cap back and as the blood flowed down his face, his eye's still held that gaze with me. I give that nigga mad respect because he held it down even while facing death. I stood there as

Krazy took Smooth's shackles off so I could carry his lifeless body outside. We placed him in the car on top of the plastic wrap where Krazy took the chainsaw and began to cut and packaged him up.

After shipping off the majority of Smooth's body part, we went to Liyah's house and dropped off a note attached to a special box. With Smooth checked off our list, we drove off knowing that we had plenty of time to prepare for the next stage in our plan.

<u>Sweetz</u>

I woke up this early morning well rested. This has been the first time in a while since I woke up and felt so good. I walked down the steps and opened the door to get the mail, only to see a brown box with a note attached to it. I kneeled down and grabbed the note only to see numbers written all over it. I yelled into the house for the girls and showed them the note. "Do any of ya'll know what this means?" I yelled. "Shit looks like coordinate numbers to me." Liyah replied. "Why the fuck would someone send a package with coordinates?" Cashmere asked with attitude. "Who gives a fuck? Just open the damn package so we can see what it is!" Tanya snapped. "Fine." I sighed, looking at them for a minute before opening the package.

I instantly flew back in shock and started to

scream from the horror I just witnessed. Inside was the head of the infamous Smooth! His head was cut off so clean; it was looked like something from the movies. It was just too unreal to me. Who could have done this? No one in New York was stupid enough to do this. Only one person would do some shit like this. Someone who was highly skilled at making hits like this. Someone like Krazy. That was when I knew it was her, she was out and she was coming for every single one of us... one by one. I stood up and went inside the house tuning out all of the other the girls screams and cries. Without hesitation, I locked myself in my bedroom and began to just wait for her to come. My time was coming...

Liyah

Tension was at an all-time high between all of us, as the search for the rest of Smooth's body parts commenced. While the police were discovering Smooth's chopped up limbs all over the city, we were busy trying to cover our asses from whoever was after us.

Once all of Smooth's body parts were discovered, we cremated his remains and decided to still have a funeral out of respect. Although I hated that nigga, he was still my blood. First our father, then my little brother Killa Mike and now Smooth. This game has no mercy on anyone. There are only two ways out this shit. You either go out in handcuffs or get put six feet under.

A single tear strolled down my cheek as I stood there and watched Smooth's ashes scatter off into the Atlantic Ocean. The crazy thing was, that with all the death and tragedy I've been surrounded by, this was the only tear that I've shed since being affiliated with the Hot Boyz.

I looked over to Mi'quel, so young and innocent. Oblivious to this event being his father's funeral. All I could do was pray that he would never get affiliated with the street life, and that at least one of us would still be surviving while he grows up. I had to figure out a way to keep us all safe because I knew that whoever was after us would show no mercy. Since Smooth was the first to go, I knew that I would be next, it's just a matter of time.

Tanya

As soon as Smooth's funeral ended, it was time for me to take the kids back to the house. I pulled up in the driveway, when I noticed that the front door was slightly open. I told the kids to stay in the car and I would be right back. I pulled my gun out the glove compartment and walk towards the house. Whoever was up in this bitch was not going to take my ass without a fight. Taking quiet but cautious steps, I looked around the living room , the kitchen, and even the den. Yet, there was no one to be found. Who the fuck is up in here? And where the fuck were they hiding?

I clinched my gun as my heart rate increased rapidly. I never was the killing type, but I wasn't about to back down this time. The sound of the car alarm going off outside caused me to jump out of instinct. I turned around and headed towards the front of the house only to see Skipper standing in front of the closed front door. I couldn't believe my eyes. Were they playing tricks on me? I thought this bitch was locked up, so why is she in my fucking house?

"How the fuck you get here Skipper?" I asked in disbelief. "Aww I thought you miss me sis? Is that the greeting I get after I held it down for you and you fucked my man in return?" She asked, as she laughed like a maniac. " Fuck you bitch!" I yelled out in anger. "That would be my pleasure." She smiled. Although I was still in shock of her presence, I went to aim my gun but Skipper beat me to the punch.

Liyah

As Cashmere and I finally made it back to the crib, I quickly noticed that Tanya's car wasn't in the driveway. From that moment, I knew something wasn't right. A distinct odor filled my nose as we walked into the house, only to find Tanya laid onto the ground with a bullet in her head. "Fuck!" I yelled out in anger and pain. Pain from losing one of the women I was attached to, and anger from someone killing off each and every one of us. This shit is getting real and I can't put my finger on who is gunning for us.

Smooth, then Tanya... who is next? I've had this shit mapped out for years, but never did I think of someone coming to kill us off. There has to be something that I'm missing. So many thought were on my mind as I looked around, only to find that the kids were missing. Better yet, where the fuck was Sweetz?

"Maybe Sweetz took the kids after finding Tanya's body." Cashmere suggested, as I sat in my office trying to think of my next move. " Then why wouldn't she call us Cashmere? Huh? C'mon, that just don't make no sense." I snapped. She rolled her eyes in disgust. "Whatever, I'm trying to think of the best out of this fucked up situation. What we need to do is get the fuck out of this house. Not be up in this hot ass spot like some sitting ducks, ready to get killed." Cashmere continued.

"I need to find the kids. Then we can get the fuck out of here." I said, as I grabbed my gun, that was taped under my desk. "You can do that shit by yourself. I don't have time to be chasing some damn kids all over town." Cashmere shrugged as she played with her acrylic nails. "Matter of fact, I need to escape from this crazy ass shit. I never thought it would get so deep like this. So I'm about to clear my head. And if the motherfucker wanna kill me, then they would have to do that shit in broad mothafuckin' daylight, cause I'm going shopping!" Cashmere ranted. I couldn't believe the dumb ass shit pouring out of her mouth. How dare she think about shopping at a time like this!

"What type of shit are you on?" was all I could say. "My mothafuckin' nephew is missing, and you thinkin' about shopping? These kids could be fucking dead right now and you over here wasting my fucking time thinking about taking yo' busted ass shopping?" I yelled in anger of her stupidity. " You think I give a fuck about those kids? Man, fuck them kids! I don't give two shits about Smooth's son, Krazy's son or anyone else's kids for that matter. I don't even like their fuckin' parents. So why would I be loyal to some damn kids that ain't even mine?

You got me fucked up!" She screamed. All I could do was stare at her before I got up and smacked the shit out of her.

"Fuck you!" Cashmere yelled out in response. " Naw, get the fuck out my face talking that reckless ass shit. I don't need none of this right now Cashmere. Just go do you, and get ya' head back' in the game. We all we got right now and you got ya' fuckin head in the clouds. If you need a release then you do that. But make sure you get it together quick cause I need you to bring that ass back with your head back in the game. Aiight?" I explained. "Whatever." Cashmere ended, before walking out the room. I sat back in my seat in disbelief. How could everything, that was once so well planned, be falling apart right before my eyes?

<u>Gutta</u>

Krazy and I rode around the Meatpacking District in Manhattan looking for Cashmere. I linked up with a few of my sources out here to keep tabs on her for a while, and this is where they said she would be. The plan was in full motion. The streets were on high alert after I killed Smooth so the ball was in our court. No one would think that this was a hit job, they would believe it was a drug on drug crime. Since he was a flashy type of dude he had a lot of nigga's who envied him and wanted him out the game, so no one would have suspected that someone from his past would have knocked him off.

"Aye I think that's her right there at the corner." Krazy pointed out, quickly snapping me out of my thoughts. I looked over only to see that broad Cashmere. "Yeah, that's her go 'head and get in the back baby." I commanded. Krazy laid down in the back of my all white range rover. I whipped around the corner, pulling right in front of Cashmere who was too busy looking down at her phone texting someone.

<u>Cashmere</u>

I looked up from my phone and laid eyes on a face that I thought I would never see again... the notorious Gutta. He sat there in his all white range rover looking like a real boss, just like I remembered him. His dreads hung down past his shoulder blades looking like a lion's mane. While his sexy chocolate brown eyes sent chills down my spine, and the way he licked those soft lips made me leak like a faucet. Damn he was just too sexy for his own good.

I walked up to him smoothing out my lime green crop top that showed off my flat stomach, paired with my skin tight zebra print leggings that flaunted my deep southern curves. My fresh off the shoe rack Giuseppe six inch heels clicked onto the ground as I walked up to his passenger window. I looked at him up and down as my pussy instantly got wet. Damn he was so fine in his crispy white V-neck, all black jeans, with ice around his neck and wrist that was so cold, it just sparkled in the sunlight.

"What's good wit you ma? It's been a minute huh?" Gutta spoke with his sexy ass voice. "It sure has" I smiled. " So what brings you out here? Last time I heard from you, you got locked up." I asked.

" Well you know, I served my time and got out a long time ago. I own a couple of businesses out here, you know, I'm trying to keep out of the gang life, trying to turn a new leaf." Gutta answered. "I feel you honey." I replied, giggling like a schoolgirl. I couldn't even act calm and cool like I wanted to. There was something about Gutta that just made me feel like I was a young girl with a high school crush.

Only Gutta could bring out that side of any woman.

"So how long you been living out this way?" Gutta asked, snapping back into my harsh reality. "For some months now." " You and yo' man?" He posed, causing me to blush. "I don't have a man. I'm still single." "Foreal? Damn why not ma? I know life obviously been treating you good. I figured yo' man has got to be doin' you right?" Gutta continued. " Are you tryin' to hit on me Gutta?" I asked, with a smile on my face. "Never that just giving a compliment when its needed." Gutta smiled back, causing me to melt right there.

" So what about you, is there a lady in your life?" I asked, reversing the subject. "Not at all. After we split, me and Krazy didn't work out either. So I was on my solo dolo shit, and still on my solo shit." Gutta answered. "Mmmhmm, I told you that it wasn't going to last." I added. "I know sweetheart I should have listen to you, but if you ain't doing nothing how about you roll with me like the good ole' days. I have to pick up this shipment at the warehouse but after that I can be all yours." Gutta suggested. I stood there, briefly thinking for a moment if I should go or not. Yet, I knew my days were numbered, might as well get some good dick out the deal! "Sure. If you're not doing nothing anyway, and you can be all mine, then why the fuck not?" I said, as I opened the car door.

I slid into the front seat and placed all of my shopping bags in front of me. I looked over at Gutta and gave him a smile before sitting completely back in my seat, relaxing as he pulled off. Excitement oozed through my body as we began our driving adventure. I haven't seen this man since I was in high school and now it's about to go down. I couldn't even sit here in silence, there was so much to discuss. As soon as I was about to ask him some questions, I felt something out of nowhere tighten around my throat. I touched my neck and felt a rope gripping onto my skin. I tried with all my might to pry it from around my neck, yet I began to feel weak. My eyes became watery as I struggled to breath. Everything seemed to just blur and then everything went black. I heard voices that was so faint I couldn't recognize who they were. Did Gutta set me up? No... he couldn't have. Why would he want to set me up? He was the one that left me, I should be the one wanting to set him up if anything….

Flashback:

I walked down the street heading towards the bus stop so I could go back to my parents' house. The tears just kept rolling down my face as I sat there and thought about what just happened. I lost everything because of that bitch! My crib, and my man, why couldn't she just be happy with Kris? Why did she have to take what was mine? I hate her! I swear one day I'mma kill that hoe…Man fuck killing

her! If I ever get the chance I will take everything
away from her one by one.

I wiped the tears from my eyes as I looked up
and noticed a man walking off a celebrity sized
charter bus that had the name "Big Meech" across
the side like he was a big time rapper. The
mysterious man strolled over to me with a great
sense of power, as his tricks followed behind him
draped in the finest clothing you can think of, and
jewelry glittering in the sunlight. He stopped in front
of me and seem so sweet and nice.

"Hey sweetie why the long face?" The man
asked. "I'm good" I replied. "Well a nice young lady
like you shouldn't be looking so down." The man
smiled. "I said, I'm good!" I snapped in annoyance.
"You don't talk like that to Big Meech you need to
have some respect bitch!" One of his tricks glared at
me. "Calm down Moscato." Big Meech leveled with
her. "I'm sorry." She said as she looked down. "It's

ok sweet thang." He caressed her face to show his sincerity. I was intrigued by the sweet side that this powerful man revealed to me.

"So where are you heading to?" Big Meech asked, turning his attention back to me. "Back to my house." I answered innocently. "Well I want to offer you a chance of a lifetime. See these lady's right here, are models and I'm taking them to L.A. to meet with one of my business partners that's going to make them famous." He explained. "Oh really?" My eyes lit up. "Yes ma'am, and just from looking at you I know that you are going to be a star." He smiled. "Yeah right" I rolled my eyes. "I'm foreal. We mean business over here and I will do all I can to back you." Big Meech ensured as he handed me one of his business cards.

I looked over the business card and it look legit, I look up at Big Meech sizing him a bit and I must say he stuck true to his name he was tall around 6ft, *black as the pavement, and was bigger than Biggie Smalls. He was a very ugly man but he had the connections, so why not. Unfortunately, I did the one thing that I would regret later and that was leaving with Big Meech to L.A. That was a rough couple of months in my life, as if I sold my soul to the devil. He had me prostituting and snorting all types of drugs. My body seem to shrink and my face turned from young to old.*

One night, I was staggered around the streets of L.A. in the midst of my high, looking for my next john. If I don't meet my quota Big Meech was going to beat my ass! As I walked around, all the city lights became distorted. I was so damn high, that I didn't even notice the man in front of me. My head started to spin, which caused me to bump right into him before passing out.

This generous man help me get into his car, and took me to the hospital where they set me up on a detox medication. I was strapped down to the hospital bed all night, sweating and have nightmares. Early the next morning I woke up in a room that was so bright. Everything that was once blurry was now clear! I looked around the room and that's when I laid my eyes on him, the man from last night. He was so fine and young I couldn't believe he stayed the night with me. This was something different the last man that showed me that type of affection was Gutta.

I looked at him as he woke up and look into my eyes. He greeted me with a priceless smile, and from that point on, I got clean and started a new life. I shared this new life with the man that helped me overcome the dark times that I was having, and his name was Jake. He was my new love, the one I showed my true self to, someone who was all mine and wouldn't be taken away from me. Finally, I had someone I loved and they actually loved me back. I felt like I was living a fairy tale with my Prince

Charming, but that all changed once I got that disturbing phone call.

"I got some bad news for ya," the voice of Kris traveled through my phone. "Killa' Mike is dead." He announced and without any hesitation I packed up my stuff and booked a flight.

I sat looking outside the window as the pilot of the plane voice boomed through the speaker " Welcome to Michigan. We will be landing at Metro airport in just a few moments." I sighed heavily as I buckled my seat belt in response. Coming back to this hell hole had my stomach doing flips. As I transition myself into the airport, I quickly grabbed my luggage and the first person I laid eyes on was Liyah.

"What's up Cashmere? I see L.A. been treating you good." Liyah greeted me with a huge smile planted on her face. "Yeah, it has." I giggled. "You're just as beautiful as always." She commented, while *she was licking her lips.*

I stood there; trying to fight back the smile on my face as Liyah grabbed some of my luggage, as well as my hand and led me outside to her car. I sat in the passenger seat as she pulled off. She gently began to stroke my thigh, causing me to get excited. I sat back in the seat and enjoyed her hands, as she started to fill me in on what's been going on since I left. I swear this moment brought back all the memories of me and Liyah. We use to have the most amazing sex even during the times when we allowed Gutta to join us.

"You know that Krazy fucked up that hit and got Gutta locked up right?" Liyah instigated. "What?" I yelled in shock. "Are you fucking serious, how could she fuck up a hit that was basically all mapped out by Kris?" I continued as

173

I jumped up in the seat. "Well you know a nigga got in the way. Feelings got her all clouded and she started fuckin' up when it boils down to business" Liyah laughed. "Well that's what their bitchasses get for fucking me over." I smirked, as I folded my arms and looked out the window.

"Yeah, that was some fucked up shit that they did to you. To make matters worse, that bitch is back up in Kris's face like nothing ever went down between her and Gutta." Liyah continued. I rolled my eyes in disgust at the thought of Krazy.

"I swear that bitch deserves everything that's coming to her!" I spoke with spite. "Shit if I was you, I would make sure that it happens." Liyah suggested, causing my hateful thoughts to flourish. "Hmm." I pondered out loud. "You might be right about that. But I just don't know what to do. You know everyone and their mama is

scared to even get close to Krazy." I said,
keeping it real with Liyah. Yet, Liyah was not
having it. "Shit fuck that! You know I got yo' back.
Just do what I say and I promise you that
everything will fall into place. Once we are done,
you will have everything that bitch has ever taken
from you."

I sat there for a moment and thought about
what Liyah said. The electricity of excitement
sprinted throughout my body at the mere thought
of revenge. This was going to be my moment to
get this bitch back for everything she did to me!
All of the hurt and pain she caused me over the
years. All of the tears I cried every night, and my
old life that was taken from me, was all going to
happen to Krazy but ten times worse! A smile
crept over my face as I looked into Liyah's eyes
and nodded my head in agreement. "Let's give
that bitch what's coming to her," was all I said to

Liyah to seal our deal. From that point forward,
our plan came into full effect.

*   *   *

I finally regained my consciousness, only to find myself in the middle of a room, strapped to a chair. My throat was throbbing and the skin around my neck burned from the previous grip of the rope. I looked around trying to see if anyone was there when all of a sudden a bright spotlight burned my eyes. I turned my head and squinted my eyes to shield myself from the brightness, when a tall figured made its way across the room and stood towering over me. I look up to see the devilish grin of Gutta.

"What the fuck is you grinning for mothafucka!" I yelled, while straining my voice. "I'm grinning at how gullible you still are." He said nonchalantly. "So I take it you are the one killing everyone off!" I questioned, as Gutta stooped down to be on my level. "Naw sweetheart, you can just think of me as an assistant." After he said that I saw another figure sashaying up to me. My eyes widen in fear because I knew that walk a mile away.

I never thought that she would get out and come so hard like this. I was so at ease since our last meeting, that I was sure that she would never see the light of day again. But, I had overlooked Krazy's power, and now I'm sitting here looking at the person that has the ultimate control of my fate; and that fate was death. Being in this situation right now, I completely understand when people say that you can't cheat death, 'cause death was knocking at my door, and the grim reaper was there to take my soul for all the sins I committed.

Krazy showed no mercy as she repeatedly beat me with the butt of her gun. "This is for all the shit you put me through!" She yelled, while dropping her gun and punching me dead in my nose. She stepped back, rubbing her fist while ranting, "You came to my cell and mocked me! You really believed that I wouldn't come for your triflin' ass! You and your bitch plotted against me and took my son and thought there wouldn't be any repercussions?" I spat out the blood that was filling in my mouth just so I could be able to reply. "You are the one that took something from me! You walk around like you was God's gift to earth! No one never took me seriously, even when I left the state to escape your shadow and I actually found a little bit of happiness, you swooped in and took that too!"

All of a sudden, Krazy burst into an uncontrollable laugh, "You really are a gullible bitch you know that?" "That little happiness you thought was so real was all orchestrated by Liyah." She continued. Tears formed in my eyes just from the thought of the first women I fell in love with could be the one to betray me like that. "That's not true!" I choked out in between sobs.

"Oh yes it is sweetie, you was just another piece to the puzzle to this whole plan. See I wouldn't expect a rookie like you to understand the minds of a real gangsta, but let me fill you in on something. She needed you because of the hatred you had for me to help stir things up. She had you guys working for Smooth to take my son from under my nose, and she knew that I would come and knock off her brother for that reason. Then she would look like a sad distraught sister who saved the day. You get it now, you was just another pawn!"

Krazy's words flowed through my mind as I tried to connect the dots. "You are lying! This is just another one of your sad sick ways to fuck with me! Liyah loved me and would never do anything to betray me." I yelled in frustration, but Krazy just stood there and shook her head like she pitied me.

"You are in so much denial that it's sickening. Jake and Jayden were Smooth and Liyah's half-brothers! Liyah had Jake pretend to fall in love with you, don't you get it Cashmere she used you!" She explained, causing my heart to break.

I sat there with tears streaming down my face as Krazy walked up and began to gag me. I had no energy to fight them anymore, I just wanted to die and leave this pathetic earth filled with liars and death! Krazy and Gutta repositioned me onto the floor as they started to torture me. By the time she was finished, my vision was so blurry that I couldn't even make out if Gutta or Krazy was still in the room. My head pounded in pain and I couldn't even open my left eye. I laid on the cold cement floor crying, just wanting it to end.

Liyah

Hours passed and Cashmere still hasn't come home. The mall was closed by now so what the fuck is going on? Without hesitation, I grabbed my phone and dialed Cashmere's number for twentieth time. Finally someone picked up the phone. "Where the fuck you been? I been calling you and you finally want to pick up the fuckin' phone hoe? I know you're not out there fuckin' some dirty broad." I began yelling into the phone, only to be laughed at in response.

"What the fuck you laughing at?" I said angrily. "Oh you don't recognize my voice Mr. Big daddy. I see you're stored in her phone as Big Daddy, so I guess you're doing big things Liyah." The female voice replied. The only person who called me Liyah was Smooth, and clearly that nigga was dead. All the

females called me Big Daddy, and the only one who would call me by my government name would be...
"Krazy! What the fuck are you doing on Cashmere's phone? What the fuck are you doing out of prison?"

"What, you thought I was going to be locked up forever? You must of forgot who I was out here on these streets. Seems like you have some miscalculations in your plan huh Liyah?" Krazy laughed. "You think this shit is funny?" I spat. "Oh it will be. Believe me." Krazy replied confidently. "Fuck you bitch!" I snarled. "Oh, you don't want to say that, especially when I got your bitch tied up, beaten to a pulp. Is that how you want to treat the one who has the power to get rid of her at any second?" I could hear her smiling through the phone. That bitch had the upper hand.

"What do you want yo'?" I asked, finally giving into her plan. "You follow these directions and you will get to see your little lover..." Krazy began to explain. I listened closely and wrote down the address of the warehouse that she wanted me to drive to.

After we got off the phone, I began to get dressed, better yet prepared, as I grabbed my guns out of the suitcase I kept hidden under my bed, and placed them in my boxers. I laced up my timberlands that enclosed my two switchblades inside my socks, and tucked my razors under my tongue. I was ready for whatever, and ready to take this bitch out and get what's mine... My lover.

I hopped in the car and sped down the interstate with my mind racing all over the place. Everything was planned out perfectly from the moment I pitched the plan to Smooth to take out Kris, Sweetz, and Krazy. I even persuaded him to let Cashmere be a part of the team to get them out. We had this shit

183

mapped out way in advanced. FUCK! How could this plan be unraveling like this?

My thoughts were broken as I pulled up to the abandoned warehouse. I hopped out of the car and swiftly made my way to the warehouse door. I pulled my guns out just to be ready, 'cause once I open this door it's no telling what was about to go down. I slid the doors open only to be greeted by Cashmere laying in the middle of the warehouse with a spotlight on her, her mouth was gagged and she was tied up. I started to walk towards her and notice she was badly beaten. One of her eye was so swollen that it was protruding out of her skull. I saw the tears running down her face when out of nowhere a gunshot rang throughout the building and she was gone!

Krazy strutted into sight with a smile of pure joy. Hurt and anger rumbled in the pit of my stomach as my lover laid there lifeless, while this bitch just stood there by her body with motherfucking smile! I instantly started to pop my guns as Krazy ran for cover. I emptied both clips as tears cascaded down my face.

I threw the guns to the floor as I screamed Krazy's name. She stood up from behind a crate looking unfazed by the shots fired from my guns. I pulled out my switchblades from my socks as a motion for her to bring everything she got, and with that it went down. She ran at me full force with a steel pipe; I ducked down low to the ground as she swung the pipe and swiftly sliced one of her legs causing her to fall. I climbed top of her and sliced the side of her face to the white meat. She screamed out in pain as her hand felt around for the steel pipe. I dug my blade into her gut causing her to cough up blood. I stared into her eyes, knowing that this was too easy and just as that thought ran through my head; I felt a bullet fly threw my chest. I gasped for air as I fell back onto the ground. As I looked up, I saw a tall silhouette hovering over me, the only thing I was able to choke out was a "fuck you" before all I could see was darkness.

Gutta

Cleaning up behind our trail would have to wait until Krazy was taken care of. Although Liyah is dead, the little bitch did put up one hell of a fight, going out like a 'G like her brother. Krazy sat in the passenger seat holding her gut in pain as I rushed her to back to Pistol's house, where he had his private on-call doctor ready to sew Krazy back up. After an emergency operation Krazy laid in here bed fast asleep. I stood there watching over her before

Pistol called me out of the room.

"I just got the call from Skipper saying that her and the kids are in Arizona." Pistol announced. " Fasho' now all we have to do is wait for Krazy to get back on her A-game." I stated, while leaning up against the wall. Pistol stood there with a smirk on his face " Yeah for as long as I've known Krazy she will be ready in a matter of weeks to finish this hit." I chuckled at his statement before replying "Yeah my Young Thang is a fighter! But we can use this to our advantage!" Pistol shook his head in agreement. "Exactly, letting Krazy have this time will have that bitch Sweetz shaking in her boots waiting for death."

<u>Krazy</u>

I pulled up to the house where Sweetz stayed with butterflies in my stomach. After months of recuperating from my last encounter, it was now time to fulfill my final hit on the list. I can't believe that this is it, the nightmare will finally be over, I can finally be able to rest knowing that everyone that did me wrong was dead and gone. This is where it will end, it started with Sweetz and it will end with Sweetz. I slipped out my car and made my way to the patio door, I looked through the window and saw that all of the lights was off except a dim light that seem to be coming from a room upstairs. I cut the alarm system wires, swiftly opened the back door and walked towards the staircase when all the lights suddenly flew on.

I cocked my gun and looked over to my left, only to see Sweetz standing in the doorway that led into the den area looking like she had lost it. I aimed my gun straight towards her head, ready to pull the trigger, but I stop myself and look at this person that stood before me, who used to be my best friend. Her once childlike face had aged dramatically. She had bags under her eyes and the hair that was always done was now matted. I lowered my gun as I looked into her bloodshot eyes drenched from tears.

"I knew you would come" Sweetz said nonchalantly, I look at her and confidently replied "Yeah I know". Sweetz took a couple steps toward me mockingly "So this is it huh Simone?" "Yea this is it." I said, while gripping the gun in my hand. Sweetz snapped and yelled at me. "Don't pull that cold hearted shit with me Simone. How can you sit there and act like it doesn't bother you?" "Cause Sweetz it doesn't, the Sweetz I once knew is dead and gone, and the person that stands before me is a stranger in my eyes." "That's Bullshit!" Sweetz yelled furiously.

"You never knew me, All you cared about was you and Kris this, and you and Kris that. Not once how Sweetz felt. You took everything from me!" Sweetz choked on the last sentence, like just the mere thought of it was a nightmare. "I ain't took a damn thing from you, everything you lost was by your own hands!"

Sweetz grabbed at her heart like she had just been stabbed by a dagger, "Are you serious? You honestly believe that it was my fault! It was because of you that I couldn't keep my child!" She said while pointing her finger at me. "My child was conceived with love between me and the man that I cherished." Sweetz's face was filled with rage as she continued. "You didn't deserve someone with all that power, You was selfish and didn't respect someone of his status." She laughed as she spoke about the only thing that I regretted the most. "Shit you didn't even cherish the seed he planted within you, You was reckless and dumb and lost the very thing that you took from me. That was supposed to be me having his first born not you! Shit not even that bitch La'Tanya deserved to have his child."

"You are delusional Sweetz! Listen to yourself. You let a man that wasn't even yours come in between us! How could you want a man that lied to you just to reach the top, not caring who he crushes just to get there." I screamed at Sweetz trying to make sure every word I said hit home. Yet ,Sweetz cut me off " HE LOVED ME THAT'S WHY!" She continued yelling, while pointing at herself. "He didn't care about you or La'Tanya. He always loved me!"

I look at my sad disheveled friend and spoke to her with as much pity as I had in my voice. " No Sweetz he didn't, he loved his power, You was just a pawn in his game of chess, can't you see that? Can't you see how he used all of us to get to the top? He was obsessed with power and look where it got him!" Sweetz sobbed, choking out her words " I can't take this anymore, I can't live without him, I can't even breathe, Not even Smooth can replace the heart I lost when Kris died. How can you stand there and act like you don't miss him?"

"Because the love I had for Kris was long gone after I found out the truth, the truth about his motive. He did love me a long time ago when he was young and innocent, but these streets killed the innocence that he had." I simply said, as I stood there and looked at Sweetz holding herself, while crying in agony. I felt the pain she felt drifting throughout the hallway. I actually felt sorry for the girl. She leaned up against the wall, slid down to the floor, and started to rock back and forth. She cradled herself like a mother would cradle their newborn child.

"Why can't I just be happy? What is the purpose of even living if the person you love isn't here. I have nothing, nobody loves me or cares about me." Sweetz's voice suddenly changed. "That's why I wanted the kids... They're so sweet and innocent; they can't help but love me. I could have given them a life that I always wanted."

"No Sweetz you couldn't have gave them what they wanted, you took them from their parents. You can never take the place of someone's parent!" I started to yell just thinking about my son and the sick and twisted delusion Sweetz had of giving him a life as his mother.

"TELL ME HOW MANY NIGHTS LIL JAKE CRIED OUT FOR ME! HOW MANY NIGHTS DID HE CRY OUT FOR HIS MOTHER?" I yelled while dropping the gun, I walked over to her snatching her off the floor shaking her violently. "How could you take my son away from me? He was mine! Everything we went through together, how could you betray and stab your best friend in the back like that?"

Sweetz laughed with glee "It doesn't matter cause I'm his mother now!!! And everything that everyone cherished is now mine! Everything that was taken from me is now mine. Don't you get it Simone?" She announced. I smacked Sweetz so hard that spit flew out of her mouth. I smacked her repeatedly with every ounce of anger I had.

I couldn't believe this chick. How could she feel that she could replace me as my son's mother? How could she let herself go so far off the deep end like that? I dropped her to the floor as she held the side of her face. She looked at me with pure hatred in her eyes while she stood up slowly, her hands were in a fist and her body trembled all over. I took a couple of steps back as her chest started to heave in and out at a rapid rate. She lunged at me as I dove for my gun. She grabbed my legs dragging me away, while I kicked as hard and fast as I could to get her off me.

She quickly pinned me down to the floor and started to choke me while crying out. "I hate you, I hate you! You took everything away from me! I can't stand you!"

I clawed at her hands that were around my neck while gasping for air, my eyesight started to blur. I knew I was going to black out soon so with the last bit of strength I had left, I reach for my gun and grasped it in my hands, and cold clocked her in the head, sending her down to the floor. I grabbed my neck gasping for air and scrambled to my feet, as I aimed my gun to her head.

Sweetz laid there holding the sides of her head screaming to the top of her lungs like she was possessed. "Get outta my head! I can't take it anymore I want it to be over with. I want to be happy just kill me! KILL ME, KILL ME, KILL ME!" She exclaimed in pure agony. Tears filled my eyes as I looked at the once confident Sweetz that could put a smile on anyone's face. The friend I used to tell all my secrets to, the one I came to for advice, the one shoulder I used to cry on when there seemed to be no hope. I couldn't. I just couldn't go through with this.

"Sorry Sweetz, I just can't." I said apologetically while lowering my gun. Sweetz looked at me and spoke in a pleading tone "Please just do it!" "No I can't Sweetz!" I shouted, while crying hysterically. "Don't you understand? It has to be you. It started with you and it has to end with you." Sweetz said in a calm tone of voice, as she stood up and walked over towards me.

She embraced me with a hug, and I could feel her body that already seemed to be cold, like she was already dead. I struggled to get her off, me but she held onto me tighter as the tears cascaded down her face. She grabbed my hand and forced the gun into her stomach and whispered in my ear goodbye as she helped me pull the trigger....BOOM

I hovered over the lifeless body of Sweetz, my last and final tie to the Hot Boyz. When Sweetz died so did Krazy, the innocent girls who got hurled into this violent and sickening lifestyle. The pain that I had for killing the one who was supposed to be my best friend would remain in this room, and once I left I would diminish the memories that I once had in this chapter of my life. I grabbed my can of spray paint that I had in my pocket and sprayed "Death to the Hot Boyz" on the wall, to make it look like a gang related homicide. I took one last look at Sweetz before I made my way to the door. This shit was finally over just as I wanted it to be.

Making a quick exit into the black night, I hopped into the black car that Gutta was waiting in. "You ready?" He asked as he nervously looked at me. "Ready as I'll ever be." I replied, as I grabbed my duffel bag from the backseat. It was time for a new change in our lives. All the blood, sweat, and tears from living in a world full of lies and betrayal was coming to an end. It was time for us to sit back and relax. We were ready to live a low key life and enjoy our peace.

*   *   *

Just as we desired, years passed by and Gutta and I lived our low key life in Arizona. Jake and Mi'quel were back in our custody, and even though my history with Mi'quel's parents was unforgivable, that doesn't mean that their son has to be punished for it. I loved him, and will continue to raise him like my own. As well as the new addition to our family, my two twin daughters, Egypt and Israel that I share with Gutta.

After closing that chapter in my life, I'm truly enjoying this new one of love and family. Something I never genuinely had. As long as I keep my two boys off the streets and not follow the paths of their father's, then my mission here on earth be will completed; But only time will tell...

"Everyone had many secrets...but Krazy only had one."

Taking a blast to the past, Tears of a True Hustler will show you what really went down while Kris and Smooth went to Atlanta. Although she was devoted to her savior Kris and her best friend Sweetz, could Krazy really be devious enough to hold the ultimate betrayal of them all? Find out what really happened in "Tears of a True Hustler"

COMING SOON!